For a Lifetime

Valerie Kapp

About the Author

Valerie A. Kapp grew up in Richland, Pennsylvania, a small town surrounded by Amish farms and a community where your parents knew what you did that day before you got home for supper. She is the oldest of five, with four younger brothers, one deceased. She had a grandfather who was blind and an uncle who was severely developmentally delayed. So no wonder her career was helping people as a counselor, specializing in counseling with the deaf. For forty years, she has lived in a suburb of Dayton, Ohio, where she is retired after working in the fields of deafness, HIV/AIDS, and vocational rehabilitation. She ended her career as a research associate at Wright State University in the Substance Abuse Resources and Disability Issues (SARDI) program. In addition, Valerie serves on the board of trustees of the Deaf Community Resource Center in Dayton, Ohio. You can find Valerie riding her Harley motorcycle, golfing with her wife and friends, visiting New York City to see Broadway plays, or every Monday night at one of their friends' houses sharing a meal and laughter.

Valerie Kapp

BELLA
BOOKS
2023

Bella Books, Inc.
P.O. Box 10543
Tallahassee, FL 32302

Printed in the United States of America on acid-free paper.

First Edition - 2023

Editor: Cath Walker
Cover Designer: Heather Honeywell

ISBN: 978-1-64247-461-9

PUBLISHER'S NOTE

Acknowledgments

I have to start by thanking my wife, Robin, who has supported me on this writing journey. And to our circle of friends for their love and laughter.

Dedication

To the pioneer lesbians who fought and confronted discrimination and oppression and dared to be themselves.

CHAPTER ONE

A loud, high-pitched beep awakens me from a dead sleep.

Beep. Beep. Beep. Pause.

Beep. Beep. Beep. Pause.

What is that noise? I inhale and immediately start coughing. And that odor?

Finally, I sit up and rub my eyes. The beeping continues. With a jolt, I realize the dense white fog is blocking me from seeing across the room.

I touch the leather underneath me to feel grounded as the fog swirls around me. If I squint, I can barely see two other high-back chairs across from me. I'm on my sister's couch in her living room. It hits me: the beeping is the smoke alarm.

Oh my God, where's Izzy?

I knock something over as I bolt across the living room. The smoke thickens with each step.

Izzy. My breath wheezes as I look to the right toward the front door, then turn left down the bedroom hallway, yelling, "Izzy, fire!" I lift the bottom of my T-shirt over my mouth and nose as my hand guides me against the wall.

Izzy's head slams into my right side as she flies through her bedroom door. "Aunt Ren—the smoke alarm—all this smoke. I'm scared." She wipes her eyes and coughs. The smoke billows down the hallway.

"We need to stay low. Let's crawl toward the front door." I lead the way, telling her to hold on to my pants leg.

I must save Izzy.

We scurry on our hands and knees down the short hallway, past the kitchen, back toward the living room and front door. I freeze in my tracks as a wave of heat attacks my face.

Orange flames climb the living room walls, devouring curtains and pictures of our Portuguese grandparents and Izzy tossing a football with her dad. The bookshelf holding my brother-in-law's construction company's awards begins to smolder. All those memories—will they survive?

The temperature rises, and the swirling smoke lurches toward us like a lion attacking its prey.

"Turn around. We need to go back," I scream as pockets of trapped steam burst from the wood stacked next to the fireplace. I push Izzy's head, forcing her to turn with me.

"It's hard to breathe," she says between coughs.

"I know. We need to hurry."

"We practiced how to get out of the house if there's a fire. If the front door is blocked, the plan"—she coughs—"is to go out the window in Mom and Dad's bedroom."

"Let's go." Both of us get as close to the floor as possible. I maneuver myself over Izzy protectively, my stomach touching her back. We go on all fours, moving like crabs toward our escape. The smoke chasing us thickens to black.

My heart pounds as my eyes continue to water. Both our coughs become loud and harsh. My throat and lungs burn.

As we make our way to the bedrooms, flames erupt from the kitchen with a *whoosh*, missing us by a few inches. I've never felt such heat. The back of my shirt feels like it's over a hundred degrees.

Izzy collapses beneath me.

"Izzy." I slap her back. "Izzy!"

"My eyes and throat hurt," she says.

"Come on, Izzy. Keep moving."

Izzy keeps crawling. We're almost at her parents' bedroom, where the hallway ends. I wonder if they've returned from shopping and firefighters are holding them back from entering their house.

"Keep moving."

The harsh smoke spirals around us, suffocating the air out of me.

"I can't breathe," Izzy says hoarsely.

I yell, "Keep moving!" I must save my niece. I wrap my arm around her stomach, holding her up so we can pick up our pace. Every breath makes my lungs hurt.

Behind us, windows explode, and snapping, hissing, and crackling sounds chase us.

We arrive at the door, Izzy coughing uncontrollably. I move my hand over the door. It's not hot, so I find the doorknob and turn it with a quick twist.

Using my knee and arm, I throw Izzy through the door opening, quickly following suit and slamming the door behind us.

We collapse onto our stomachs. The room is free of smoke. I look up and see our escape across the room, on the other side of the queen-sized bed. Our coughs become less severe, but it's still hard to breathe. I get up on my knees and stand. We don't have much time.

Izzy says, "My chest hurts."

I pull her up and wrap her in my arms. "Mine too." I wipe my runny nose. My throat is dry and scratchy. Izzy's tears make a road map on her black, soot-smeared face.

"Sirens," she gasps as a high-pitched wail gets closer and closer. I push her toward the window on the other side of the room.

When we get to the window, I open it and yell at her, "Go!"

Izzy lunges at me and wraps her arms around my neck. "What about you?"

I glance back at the door, where smoke has begun to slither in, the long gray wisps curling into darker ones. The popping and sizzling above us gets louder.

I grab her arms and pull them down to her side, looking directly into her eyes. "I'm right behind you."

With all the strength I have left, I lift her out into the fresh air.

She is safe.

I raise my leg, ready to make my escape. But instead, there is a crisp *snip-snap-whoosh*. I look up as a roaring blaze of orange, red, and yellow flames crash down.

I awaken with a scream. I'm lying in the fetal position, my hand and arms covering my head. My eyes scan the dark room, my heart racing. Sweat drenches my tank top and bedsheets.

I take a deep breath in through my nose and let it out through my mouth before uncoiling and lying flat on my back. I keep taking deep breaths and releasing them as I remind myself that Izzy is safe.

CHAPTER TWO

The following morning, I wake bleary-eyed like after most nights lately. The exhaustion is like a jacket I struggle to take off, wondering if I have the strength to make it through another day. I take a deep breath and whisper to myself, "my anniversary."

But I need to be on time. My best friend and Westwood High's curriculum director, Darlene, scheduled a meeting with a company to discuss virtual reality for the classroom.

As I drive through the staff parking lot, I wave to a couple of teachers. I pull into one of the four reserved administration spots in the front of the building.

I get out of the car just as Darlene pulls in beside me, blowing her horn. My adrenaline skyrockets, my hand flying to my heart. "What the hell was that for?"

"Wanted to make sure you're awake," she says when she steps out of her car. "Those dark circles under your eyes tell me you had a rough night."

"Well, since this meeting coincides with the sunrise, I didn't get a chance to cover my raccoon eyes." I turn to her. "Is it noticeable?"

"No. But I've seen you through the worst and best of times. By the way, that scarf goes well with your outfit."

"Thank you." I straighten my navy blue blazer as we walk through the main doors. We take the hallway through the open commons area, where students congregate during the day, then turn right to make our way to the administration offices. "You had to make this meeting this early? Six thirty in the morning?" Only Darlene would have her head on straight this early. She's always eager and enthusiastic, no matter the time of day. Unlike me, who can't get a good night's sleep to save her life.

"Yeah, that was the only time we were both available this week. And it only gives us about fifteen or twenty minutes before the department head meeting."

I blink. "Can you fill me in again? Why virtual reality? I thought it was for playing games."

Darlene rolls her eyes and sighs. "You can, but there are a lot of other applications. By the way, you can say VR instead of virtual reality."

"VR. Got it." I tap my finger to the side of my head.

"Okay, so what do you know about VR?"

"My brother-in-law, Ryan, owns a headset. Is that what it's called?"

"Yes," she says with a sly grin on her face.

"I've watched him a couple of times. When he wears the headset, he holds these handles and swings his arms in the air like the robot from *Lost in Space*."

We stop by Darlene's office, where she puts her belongings on her desk before returning to me. "*Lost in Space*?"

"Oh, I always forget that you were in grade school when I was in college. You know, the TV show with the robot waving his arms whenever there was danger? They looked like springs? Like this." I wave my arms around. "'Danger, Will Robinson, danger!'"

Darlene giggles. "No, I haven't seen that show."

"Oh, never mind. Do you have a VR? Is it a system?"

She glances at her watch. "We better head down to the conference room."

"I'm not sure I'm up for this today. This virtual rea—VR."
I hope I can focus on this meeting. This VR stuff is probably
expensive. However, I've read studies showing students'
motivation increased, but there was a need for more research
on its effectiveness in increasing test scores.

She hands me a folder. "Please keep an open mind. It's only
a preliminary meeting. And you did tell me to follow my gut
when I first mentioned this project to you."

Darlene has been insisting on having this meeting for
months. In her opinion, it could help raise our STEM scores,
which we need to do or I may not have a job for much longer.

"Keep an open mind. Please?"

"Okay. You are the curriculum director, and you're on top
of the latest trends in education." I wave at her to take the lead.
"Let's go."

The conference room is small, with a boat-shaped conference
table. Eight black nesting chairs surround it. Four people stand
as we enter.

"You're early," Darlene says.

A tall gentleman with black hair pulled back into a ponytail
says, "Hi, I'm Jared Stewart, Product and Project Manager
of JAWS. This"—he points to his left—"is Anthony Walters,
Senior Software Engineer. Next to Anthony is Sarah Reynolds,
our Marketing, Sales, and Distribution Manager. And our
president, Brianna Walsh. And before you ask, JAWS is not an
acronym for anything other than the initials of our names."

"Jared! Finally, I can put a face to a name. We've talked on
the phone a couple of times. It's nice to meet you." Darlene
turns to me. "I'd like you to meet our principal, Renata Santos."

I make sure to hold the folder in my left hand and move it
behind my back when we shake hands. When I reach toward
Brianna's outstretched hand, I notice her warm and firm grasp,
and her long fingers envelop my hand.

Brianna asks me, "Do you have a preferred seat?"

I glance at the blue of her eyes and clear my throat. "No,
please sit anywhere you like."

My eyes stay glued to Brianna as she returns to the chair at the head of the table, the chair opposite the one I take. She has thick, black, wavy hair with silver streaks.

We all take our seats, and Anthony, who wears black, oversized glasses and a wrinkled button-down, begins explaining.

"Virtual reality is a simulated experience. It can be similar to the real world or altogether different from the real world, like my favorite game in VR, *Flight Simulator*. It has a multitude of applications, such as entertainment, video games, and education. For example, the medical and military arenas use VR for training. We…"

I watch Brianna watch Anthony as he explains VR. She has a prominent chin, a slightly upturned nose, and high cheekbones. Her hair is shoulder length and parted to the side, with a few bangs falling across her forehead. When she laughs, she shows laugh lines around her mouth and crow's feet around her eyes. Her smile radiates confidence. I can't help noticing her full and enticing lips.

"Renata, did you hear the question?" Darlene asks.

I startle. "Uh—no, sorry. Would you repeat it, please?"

"Have you ever experienced VR?" Sarah asks.

"No. I've seen people use it. I've never experienced it myself. I'm not sure VR is, um, appropriate for a high school classroom." It'll be another thing to add to the already overworked staff. Not to mention the uphill battle it'll be to convince the board why we need it and then figure out how to pay for it.

I notice Brianna tilt her head.

"VR can supplement the educational environment by providing access to places and objects that students may never see otherwise," Jared says.

"So, for example, if you're in a biology class discussing cells, you can see the cells in 3-D and interact with them. Isn't that right?" Darlene asks Jared.

"Absolutely. Our company has developed apps for all subject areas, from science to math to history."

"I still don't quite understand the concept. I'm not sure about it," I hedge. This sounds expensive. I don't have money just sitting in my budget, waiting to be spent. And to top it all off, we have the school levy on the ballot. It's hard enough to convince our community to vote for a school levy that will raise their property taxes. How will the community view the cost of VR in the schools?

Brianna stands. Her shoulders are broad. Her body is somewhat overweight but firm and solid-looking. She is dressed in a purple V-neck blouse, gray pants, and a light-gray blazer. She moves behind her three colleagues and places a hand on Jared's shoulder. "I understand your hesitation. However, from my research about your school district, it is progressive and on the cutting edge of bringing in new ideas."

I scoot my chair back from the table. "Yes, we have that reputation."

"So, imagine you are a geology teacher talking about the Grand Canyon. As you and your students walk down the Bright Angel Trail, you can point out the forty major sedimentary rock layers to them. They experience and learn about geological evolution through time without even being there."

Maybe I can disrupt the flow of the meeting so I can get out of here sooner than later. "You seem to know something about geology, Ms. Walsh," I say lightly.

She smiles. "Not necessarily. However, we do our research when developing our educational apps." She smirks and adds, "Along the way, I've realized I might not have paid enough attention when I was in high school."

I nod and smile back.

As the conversation continues, I begin tapping my finger on the table. My dream keeps popping in and out of my head, interrupting my concentration. Why are the dreams starting again? Up until a couple of weeks ago, I hadn't had one for, I don't know, a few months. I thought I was done with them. Are they trying to tell me something? I went through hell, and the dreams keep making me relive it. I want them to stop.

Sarah continues, "The students can be there instead of seeing it in a book."

I hear my name. My eyes meet Brianna's as she says, "Ms. Santos, there are studies that show a significant increase in students' enjoyment in learning science when VR is used and that the use of VR increases students' self-efficacy as well. Also, studies are beginning to show an increase in test scores because students are more confident and trust what they've learned through VR. VR provides an alternative experience to learning."

To my surprise, my heart skips a beat.

"And I can provide you the references if you would like."

Darlene interrupts, "Sorry, but we have another meeting before the students arrive. It all sounds very interesting. Can we schedule another time to continue this discussion?"

Jared replies, "Certainly. Can we find a time after your school day, so we can bring headsets for you to experience VR?"

"Sure," I say quickly. Thank God this meeting is over. "We'll get back to you with a day and time."

Everyone else stands, and Anthony says, "Thank you for your time. We look forward to demonstrating the endless possibilities of VR in an educational setting."

Brianna leans forward and extends her hand. "Nice to meet you, Ms. Santos."

Is she holding my hand longer than necessary? Did she just feel the same electric jolt? I haven't had this reaction to a woman since Maggie, and I don't remember it being this strong.

Brianna turns to Darlene and shakes her hand, after which they move out.

I follow them to my office door and scrutinize the group as they move down the hall. Sarah, who's short with wavy red hair, walks sandwiched between Jared and Anthony, a three-story building between two towering skyscrapers. Brianna follows them, her shoulders back and head lifted, straight and tall.

When she gets to the common area, she sidesteps students standing and talking, and stops. Then she turns and looks directly at me, giving me a smile and a small wave, before continuing to exit the building.

I need to keep this professional.

CHAPTER THREE

There are no surprises at the department head meeting, thank God. Of course, the English department head doodles on the back of the agenda handout, and the World Language head can barely keep her eyes open, but we get everyone's attention when we relay the board's concern with our low STEM scores. Our curriculum meets all the state testing standards—with the exception of STEM.

Afterward, Darlene and I walk back to our offices, dodging students at their lockers. "You really think this...VR can benefit the students?"

"Yes, I do," says Darlene.

"What do we know about the company?"

"They're one of the leaders in VR app development—specifically, educational apps."

"I'll need more ammunition for the board. You know, our board president, Mr. Fisher, questions every new idea, not to mention Ms. Miller, his little sidekick who follows him like a puppy," I remind her. "We'll need to have our ducks in a row when we present this. The four people today—are they partners? Ms. Walsh was introduced as the president, but Jared led the meeting."

Darlene smiles. "Oh, so you noticed her. She's good-looking for an older woman, huh?"

Too quickly, I respond, "Really? You interested?"

"No, not for me. I like blondes."

"Yeah, I know. You told me Shelly was a blonde."

"Yeah, she is, but Bri looks like your type. You like them tall. She's taller than you, confident, self-assured, maybe a little older than you—"

I interrupt, "That's true, but no."

"Don't you need to start thinking about dating again?"

I run my hand over my left arm, feeling my skin grafts. "No."

"Renata, you're attractive. You have an athletic body—"

"Sure, but I do have the beginnings of some"—I tap my belly—"belly fat."

"Oh, don't we all?" Darlene squeezes her own, grinning.

My body tenses. "Yeah? But what about what you can't see?" I turn and take a step down the hall.

She grabs my arm and turns me toward her. "People experience your kindness and passion in how you interact with everyone."

I pull my arm from her grasp. "I'm not talking about that."

"Renata, you are not your—"

"Stop." I glance around to see if students are watching—they aren't—and look back at her. "Just stop, Darlene."

She raises both her hands in surrender. "Sorry." A few steps later, she says, "Okay. Back to the VR company and the next meeting."

"Yes, find out more, and let's set up a time." I'm grateful for the subject change. "Since they're bringing headsets, should we invite a department head or two and a couple of teachers?"

"Why don't you call Brianna and ask her?"

"Ugh." I roll my eyes. "I'm not even sure of this VR stuff. What makes you think I'm the right person to talk to her at this point?"

"I am convinced VR can supplement students' learning experience. Maybe if you actually *talk* to Brianna, she could answer some of your questions before the meeting."

"You do not give up, do you?"

"Nope."

"All right. Email me the company phone number. I'll give her a call."

CHAPTER FOUR

All week, I'm bombarded with one demand after another: suspension of two students who brought marijuana into the building, a student with mental health issues, the school play on Wednesday night, and then the board meeting on Thursday night.

The board meeting went on and on about the low STEM scores.

Then there's the work to convince the community to vote yes on the school levy so we don't have to lay off staff or cut transportation. Where does it all end?

Of course, there's VR and whether it's appropriate for us to add it as a tool for learning.

I dress in a pair of jeans, my walking boots, a long-sleeved shirt, and a fleece pullover, my Saturday clothes, and head off for a walk. As I stroll down the sidewalk, I ponder my future. Maybe it's time I considered retiring. I'm not looking forward to the battle to pass another school levy, and working with some board members who are at times completely oblivious to what goes on in a school building day-to-day is frustrating as hell. I pick up my pace.

Rita, a neighbor, says hi and asks if she can join me on my walk. She has two children in high school, so as we turn the corner, I ask, "Have you heard of virtual reality?"

"I have! My oldest daughter got a headset for her birthday. She loves it."

"Really!"

As we continue to walk around the block, she explains, "She uses it to watch movies, play sports, and somehow—I don't understand how it works," she admits with a laugh, "but she went on safari in South Africa."

I stop in my tracks. "No kidding."

"Well, here I am." She stops at her driveway. "Thanks for letting me join you on your walk. I'm available anytime."

As I walk back to my house, I wonder about VR, which brings me back to Brianna Walsh and my conversation with Darlene. If I *were* interested in her, why would she be interested in me? No one would be able to look at this body and get turned on.

CHAPTER FIVE

On Monday morning, Darlene and I walk the halls between classes. The hallway echoes with lockers slamming, loud laughter, and students hustling to their classes.

Darlene asks, "Did you call Brianna yet?"

"No. I'm waiting until you have more information on the company."

"Okay, well, I found out that the four worked together at a university and did research using VR. When the money dried up, they started their own company." As we maneuver between students, she asks two of them, "Hey, Amina, hey, Rhonda—you guys ready for the debate next week?"

"Yeah, we got this, Ms. Myers," Amina says as they both high-five Darlene.

"How long have they been in businesses?" I continue when the girls turn to catch up with their friends.

"For about eight years. From what I understand, people in the field respect their work."

"Good to know."

The bell rings as we turn the corner and narrowly miss colliding with three students hurrying from the other direction. "Good morning," I say.

All three stop, eyes wide with shock, like they've been caught. "Good morning, Ms. Santos and Ms. Meyer," they respond in unison.

I check my watch. "Running a little late?"

"Um, our class is down the hall," one student answers.

"Get going then." When I smile, they do, too, relieved.

Finally, doors close, and quietness comes over the halls as we continue to our offices.

"Okay," I continue, "back to our discussion. Only the four of them?"

"No, I believe they employ about ten more programmers. Jared and Anthony are the directors of the development-programming department."

"Okay."

"According to the people I talked with, they're expanding their reach to high schools. Their systems are already used in med schools and other tertiary institutions."

"More ammo if and when we go to the board." Do I tell Darlene I did some of my own investigating last week? I might have checked out Brianna Walsh's LinkedIn account and pulled up the company website. She's quite an interesting person.

"I did find out they developed a dating app for lesbians," Darlene adds.

I stop and look at her. "What?"

"Yeah. I guess it's a virtual reality where you can go and meet other lesbians. You create your avatar and can socialize at different locations, like a coffee shop, movie, a walk, or even a hike."

"You've got to be kidding me?" I marvel. "Who would do that? It's hard enough to meet people in the real world. But now you create a fake person and meet in a made-up world? Really?"

"A friend of mine told me about it."

"You would think that, at fifty-eight years old, I would be more aware of this technology."

"We-ell," she says slowly, "you are now. So, you want to visit the dating app?"

"Darlene." Why is she pushing me to get back into dating? I only recently stopped turning away when I look at myself in a mirror.

"Yes, really, Renata. I know Maggie hurt you." She waves that aside. "Enough of that. Back to you. You deserve to meet someone who will cherish you for who you are: a kind, caring, and fun person."

"No. No way."

Darlene laughs. "Oh, come on. Take a risk. Dive into the wild side."

"Do you have a headset?"

"No."

"Well, neither do I, so how could we use the app?"

"We could ask your brother-in-law to use his," Darlene suggests.

"No. Definitely not."

"Come on, ask him."

"No. I'm not even close to wanting to share my body with anyone. I need more time."

"Oka-a-ay," Darlene says, huffing a large sigh.

"I appreciate your encouragement, but—"

She touches my arm. "I understand. I mean, I don't completely understand what you've been through, but I want you to be happy. But since the fire, you've withdrawn from socializing with new people."

"I know. I'm not ready." Am I ready to date? How would I explain what happened and how my body looks now? I don't know how to do that. And people who already know about the fire look at me with pity. I don't want anyone's pity.

"Back to work," Darlene says.

Walking back into my office I think back to my friendship with Darlene. We have been friends for over twenty years. We met at Westwood High School when I was assistant principal and she was head of the history department. I admired her passion for education and the way she would go the extra mile for the students—she always thought of the students and what was best for them, challenging the staff to find creative ways to instruct students. After she received her master's degree in education admin, I encouraged her to apply for the curriculum director job.

Our gaydar drew us together as friends. Now I don't know what I would do without her personally and professionally. She always had a knack for staying in the loop, so during my six-month recovery, she kept me informed of all the goings-on at school and the school board. On days I felt down, she never failed to surprise me with a home-cooked meal or a special treat. And any time I needed her moral support for doctor's appointments or physical therapy sessions, she was right there beside me, cheering me on.

I sit at my desk, looking out the window overlooking the courtyard. Should I start dating? It's been almost three years—since Maggie left me. Why am I thinking about this? Why start, why risk another rejection?

What I need to do is call Brianna and schedule our next meeting. VR just might provide the tool to raise our STEM scores.

My desk is free of clutter. My computer makes it possible to do everything for which I'm responsible as principal. So, I guess technology has a role. Maybe VR does too.

As I contemplate calling Brianna, my phone rings. "Ms. Santos, how can I help you?"

"Good morning, Ms. Santos. Brianna Walsh here."

I sit up straighter in my chair. "Ms. Walsh. Good morning."

"How are you today?"

"Fine, thank you. Yourself?"

"Doing great, thanks. I was wondering if you have a few minutes to talk about VR?"

"Sure."

"From our meeting last week, I sensed your hesitancy about VR being a tool in the educational setting, so I'm wondering if I can meet with you to discuss it further." Her voice is clear and light, engulfing me in a feeling of warmth.

"I was just getting ready to call you to schedule that demonstration we discussed."

"Oh, you were? Good. But I think it would be more useful if you and I could meet one-on-one. You seem reluctant, and I can give you a hands-on demonstration of how the system works."

I turn and stare out the window. "With just you?"

"Yes, well—I think a personal demonstration would give you a solid understanding of how the system works before meeting with your colleagues. They will look to you for guidance. You don't want to be seen as uninformed, do you?"

I nod, even though she can't see me.

"And you can ask me any questions you may have about our company." There's a pause before she continues, "Look, Ms. Santos, I respect your concerns about whether VR is advisable, or perhaps congruent, with a high school curriculum."

"I'm not necessarily saying that," I try. That's exactly what I'm saying. "I mean, I trust Darlene."

"I know Darlene is excited about the possibility of incorporating VR into the curriculum."

"She is. But"—I gather my thoughts—"I agree with you that I need to understand VR to make the case to the board if we decide VR is worthwhile."

"Okay, so when can you and I meet?"

"What about Thursday afternoon—say, about four thirty?"

"I'm available," Brianna responds without hesitation. "Where would you like to meet?"

"My office here at the school."

"I'll be there." Again, no hesitation.

I stand and start to pace as far as the telephone cord allows. "Do I need anything set up for the demonstration?"

"No. You and your office will be fine."

"So, Thursday it is," I repeat.

"I look forward to seeing you again."

"Goodbye, Ms. Walsh," I mutter before hanging up.

CHAPTER SIX

The digital clock over my office door reads 4:25 p.m. Brianna still hasn't arrived. For the third time, I straighten the pictures of Anne Sullivan, Helen Keller, Bill Nye, and Christa McAuliffe hanging on my wall, then walk to my desk chair and sit.

How did I let Brianna convince me to have an individual demonstration? Maybe because I'm attracted to her?

A knock at the door pulls me back to reality. My stomach tightens as I say, "Come in."

In steps Brianna, her bright blue eyes and smile conveying reassurance, revealing dimples in her cheeks. Her smile captivates me. I find myself holding my breath.

My eyes meet hers. I swallow hard and nod to acknowledge her entrance. She holds a small, black, rectangular box.

"Ms. Walsh, please come in. Can I help you with that?"

"No thanks, I got it. Can I set this on your desk?"

"Please."

"You have a very organized desk," she says, chuckling. "My work desk has folders and piles of paper scattered all over it."

"How do you find something when you want it?"

"Oh, the stacks are organized." Her laugh is calming, and my body relaxes.

"I thought you of all people would use more technology to organize your work."

"Nah, not me. I'm old-school. I like paper."

"But what about—"

Brianna steps back and raises her hands in surrender. "Before you say anything about all the trees, I do recycle."

I grin and point to the rectangular box. "I'm guessing that's the VR headset? My brother-in-law has one."

"So, you *have* seen a VR headset, at least! Good. Ms. Santos, we have a starting point."

"Please call me Renata."

"Thank you, Renata. Please call me Bri." She looks around. "Nice office. Good view into the courtyard, and it lets in natural light. She walks over to a wall with plaques. "The Ohio Association of Student Leaders' Administrator of the Year Award. Wow!" she says, her eyes bright.

"Thank you." My neck is getting hot. "I'm most proud of that one."

"Why?"

"The recognition is based on nomination from students, advisers, and other administration. It's humbling."

Bri walks to the other side of my office and points to the pictures I just straightened. "Interesting choices. Why them?"

"Well," I begin as I point to the pictures, "Annie Sullivan and Bill Nye used their ingenuity, adaptability, flexibility, and patience to create real-world learning in their teaching." Why am I talking like a robot? Relax, she's not going to bite.

"It sounds like you've memorized that."

I laugh in spite of myself. "Those are the core values of our school. I use them a lot when talking with teachers and parents, so I guess I'm on autopilot." I laugh again.

"Okay, so how about Christa McAuliffe?"

"Her courage and bravery. You know, what she did… going into space despite any fears she may have had…she's an inspiration to us all."

"You can say that again." Bri moves toward my desk and points to the plaque by the built-in oak bookcase. "What about this one?"

When I follow her, we're only inches apart. A light scent of lavender.

She leans over my shoulder and reads, "The National Distinguished School Award."

"It recognizes schools that demonstrate a wide variety of strengths."

"And the strengths would be?" She turns to me, and we're too close. I take a step back.

"Uh—the—the strengths can include implementing a team approach to teaching and learning, focusing on professional development for staff, and building strong partnerships between the school, parents, and the community. Another memorized response." Heat rises up my neck again—from embarrassment, or is it from something else? I move back to my desk. "No need to be impressed. I work with a great staff—and that includes the secretaries and janitors, who, by the way, are the backbone of a school."

"Well, don't sell yourself short. It takes strong leadership to inspire others to become their best."

Our eyes meet, and silence engulfs the room. I lower my eyes, not knowing where to look.

Finally, I clear my throat. "Enough about me. So, you're here to teach me about VR?"

Bri retrieves the headset and the two handles from the box. "I'll demonstrate how to put on the headset and how to hold the wands."

"Oh, they're called wands. I thought they were like handles."

"Close enough." She smiles, demonstrating how to put on the headset and wands before handing them to me.

I hold and turn the headset every which way, shaking my head. "It looks like a giant pair of goggles." I start to put on the headset, and I remember my hand. I stop. Inhale. I have a hole in my cuff for my thumb, so the scar on my left hand isn't visible. I exhale and start again with the headset.

"Would you like some assistance?" She steps closer.

"No, I can do it," I say quickly. But then my hair gets tangled in the straps of the headset.

"Your hair is thick. Moving your hair behind your ears might help," she says.

"No. I'll be fine," I say too loudly.

Bri raises her hands defensively and takes a step back.

I pull the headset over my head and adjust the straps. Why did I snap at her? She was only trying to help.

She instructs me on how to start the program, and then I see the directions in the headset, explaining the buttons on the wands.

"You need to create a guardian zone," she says.

"Yeah, I'm at that part now." I point the right wand at the floor, hold the trigger, and draw a circle around me, creating a guardian zone in the open space of my office.

"You're getting the hang of it, Renata."

Her voice is calming, even though I can't see her. "I hope me looking like a giant ant with bulging eyes and flapping wands doesn't compromise my reputation as a leader."

She laughs. "I doubt it. It might actually make them see you as a cool, hip leader." Then she adds, "Okay, so let's say a counselor is working with a student to determine which college they would like to attend. There's an app where the student can visit a virtual campus."

Standing in my guardian zone, I say, "That would be interesting. Can we try it?"

"Sure. Let me walk you through how to find the app."

I follow Bri's instructions, and I direct the red laser light to the Wittenberg University app and press the trigger to launch it. Before I can react to the warning, I leave the safe space and bump into my desk. A soft hand on my arm guides me gently back into the safe zone.

I straighten at her touch.

She says, "Sorry. I didn't want you to fall. I should have asked if I could touch you."

"No—thank you." *For touching me. I can't remember the last time anyone touched me.* I clear my throat. "I'm fascinated by how realistic—I mean, I'm on the campus, walking into a dorm." I look to my left, to my right, and behind me. "It's just like I'm there."

"I know, isn't it cool?"

"I mean, I make a three-sixty-degree turn and see the bed, desk, pictures on the wall, mirror—" All of a sudden, I feel dizzy and have the urge to vomit. I stick out my arms. "I think I'd better sit down."

Bri's hands are on my arms, steadying me. "Whoa—why don't you take off the headset?"

I stiffen. "Thank you." My hands shake. Is that because I feel sick or because her touch made me feel…safe?

"Um—your hair. It's a little messy by your ears. May I?" Bri asks.

She's only inches away from me. I take a step back. "Uh, sure."

She raises her hand and smooths my hair, then reaches for my left side. I quickly block her hand. "I'll do it."

She looks puzzled, but she says, "You turned too fast. It takes a while to become accustomed to the movement. May I lead you back to your chair?"

"No, I've got it. Thanks." Bri's touch felt comforting.

"So, what do you think?" she asks, standing in front of me, my desk between us.

"I mean, I enjoyed the tour of the campus before I felt sick." It reminds me of how I felt on my medication in hospital. I touch my stomach. I don't ever want to feel that way again. "I'd like to see the apps related to STEM because if they're as specific and real as the campus app, I just might swing toward VR having potential."

She smiles and says, "Sounds promising. How is your stomach now?"

"Much better, thanks." I clear my throat. "I'd like to invite some staff to a demonstration. Would that be okay with you?"

"That would be fine. How many, so I can bring enough headsets for everyone?"

"I'll ask Darlene to send you the number once we have it. Next week Thursday at four thirty again seems to be a good time. Will that work for you?"

"We will be there."

"Thank you for the, um, personal demonstration. I appreciate your time." I stand and start packing the headset into the box.

"Oh, no." Bri touches my arm. "It's yours."

When her hand stays on my arm, my muscles tense again. "What?"

As if she can read my mind, she removes her hand. "If you want more experiences between now and next week, you have a headset. Maybe your brother-in-law can give you some pointers and show you some other functions, games, and apps."

"That's generous of you. Thank you."

Her eyes show concern. "Are you feeling better?"

"Yes, thank you."

"Then I'll be here next week—Thursday," she says as she walks to the door. She stops and turns. "Ms. Santos—um, Renata—you may want to get something to eat to help with your nausea."

I suddenly decide to shoot my shot, as my students say. "Well, I need to finish some work here first, but do you have any plans later?"

"Yeah, I do. I'm meeting someone for dinner, then a movie."

My heart sinks. Does she have a partner? Or is she going on a date? It wouldn't surprise me, a successful businesswoman like her, with those blue eyes and bright smile. Who wouldn't jump at the chance to be with her?

"Okay, um, thank you for the demonstration."

"Don't forget to eat something."

"I will after I finish here." I try to broaden my smile.

"Have a nice evening, Renata."

"Good night. I look forward to our next meeting with the staff." I watch the door close behind her, then turn off my computer and grab my coat off the rack in the corner of my office. I wanted to go to dinner with her. I haven't felt the need to be with anyone for a long time but wanted to go to dinner with Bri.

CHAPTER SEVEN

I decide to ask my brother-in-law, Ryan, to teach me about VR when I join him and his family for Sunday dinner. I felt a pang of guilt—it had been two months since our last Sunday dinner together. The fire that had destroyed their house made headlines in town, so it was no surprise when Ryan's parents insisted they move in with them until they could rebuild in a new housing development a block from their old house. There was so much going on with the build, moving, and Clare and Ryan staying on top of running their construction business at the same time, there was no time. I'd stop occasionally, but not every Sunday, as had been our tradition.

I turn into the driveway of their new home and park in front of the two-car garage.

My niece, Izzy, is on the porch swing, reading a book. She is so absorbed, I beep my horn to get her attention.

Her body jerks as she raises her head. "Aunt Ren, you scared me!" she shouts, sprinting toward me.

As I step out, Izzy crashes into me, wrapping her arms around my waist and squeezing me as hard as she can. I hug her back and kiss her on top of her head.

"Are you all moved in?"

"Yeah. The house is great."

I scan the red-brick house. "Dad's construction company does outstanding work, huh?"

"Well, duh." Izzy steps back, her hands on her hips. "Dad's the boss. So it's the best."

I crack a grin. "Is Dad home yet?"

"Nope, but come in. Mom is excited you're here. She made bifanas." She pulls my arm and draws me down to whisper in my ear, "Between you and me, yours are better. But don't tell her I told you."

I laugh. "I won't." I get the black box from my back seat.

"What's that?"

"Your dad is going to show me how to do this VR stuff."

"Oh. He acts funny sometimes when he plays with the VR. Come on." Izzy grabs my hand and drags me into the house.

The aroma of the massa de pimentão, garlic, and red pepper marinade for the pork overwhelms me.

"Mom, Aunt Ren is here," Izzy yells.

"Ren! In here," Clare yells back.

Izzy leads me through the foyer into the living area, which is wide open with the sun shining through two sets of French doors leading to a lanai on the opposite side of the house. The wood floors are gorgeous, and the kitchen to the left looks like it came out of a *Better Homes and Gardens* advertisement.

It's so much different than their other house—the one that burned down.

Izzy climbs onto a stool at the island. Her mom is hovering over the stove with her back to us.

"Clare, it smells wonderful."

She turns and wipes her hands on her apron. "Come here and give your little sister a big hug."

I maneuver around the island, stop, and touch the tops of her arms before leaning in and kissing her cheek.

"I missed you," Clare whispers in my ear.

"I missed you too," I whisper back. I hope she doesn't notice the dark circles under my eyes because she'll know I'm not sleeping, and then she'll start asking all kinds of questions. Her eyes show concern as she turns back to the stove. "Are you hungry? I made bifanas."

"I can always eat bifanas, you know that."

"Mine are not as tasty as yours."

"Thanks. I don't cook a lot these days." I peek into the dining room and straighten the family picture on the wall before walking back into the kitchen area. "That blast of heat when you open the oven…still working on it."

"Hey, Aunt Ren," Izzy says.

"Yes, Izzy?"

"Uh—Mom said you had some surgery again." Izzy bites her bottom lip, staring at her hands folded on the counter.

I turn to Clare, who mouths, *She wonders why you're not visiting as much.*

"Yeah, I did. On my neck."

"I'm sorry." Her tears begin to well. "It's my fault."

"Izzy! It's not your fault." I hold her for about fifteen seconds, then turn her around to face me. "Remember the questions we talked about in family therapy?"

"Yeah," she says softly.

"What were the questions?"

"Did I start the fire?"

"And your answer?"

"No."

"Remember, the fire marshal said it was an electrical fire started by old wiring."

Izzy nods her head.

"You're the one who remembered the escape plan, right?"

"Yes. But you still got burned." She touches the scar that starts at the top of the back of my left hand and travels up my arm. "Does it still hurt?"

"Not as much anymore."

"Are you sure?"

I hold her face in my hands and look directly into her eyes. "I'm here. You're here. You are in your new home. And we are all going to have dinner together. And I bet you might find some dessert if you go to my car."

Izzy's eyes widen. "My favorite?"

"Maybe. You better go and find out."

She jumps off the stool and runs out the door. I turn and lean against the counter, close to tears.

"Ren? You okay?" asks Clare.

I straighten and turn away. "Yeah."

She grabs my left arm and I grimace.

"Sorry, did I hurt you?"

"No. It's—no one touches—I haven't—my arm doesn't usually get touched." I look up. "So I'm getting used to how it feels when it is."

"Come on. Let's sit down." Clare leads me to the couch.

The door from the garage opens. "Honey, I'm home."

In walks Izzy with Ryan, rugged with his unshaven face, a Cleveland Browns hat, and a Cargill jacket. They have cookies in their hands and crumbs on their lips.

"I see you found them," I say, laughing. And for the moment, all the bad memories are swept away.

*　*　*

After the dishes are in the dishwasher, Ryan and I go into the family room. We move two chairs so we have room for our separate guardian zones. Ryan walks me through the features of VR and gives me a refresher on how to locate the apps.

Izzy and Clare laugh as Ryan and I move our arms and turn in a circle. "They look like an octopus, waving their arms all over the place."

After we play a game, I ask Ryan, "Can we experience educational apps instead of *Star Wars*? By the way, I kicked your butt in the saber battle."

"Well, I'm used to swinging a hammer, not a saber," he says, chuckling.

Ryan directs me to the NAT GEO app and then the MEL Chemistry app. Finally, he directs me to Apollo 11, where I view Earth from outer space.

"I can't believe how real everything looks," I say, turning. "This is so cool. I'm amazed at this technology." I turn again and stagger. "Whoa, I need to sit down and take this off. I'm getting a little nauseous."

Ryan says, "Yeah, it takes time to get accustomed to the movements. For me, the nausea disappeared after a month or so."

"Brianna Walsh told me the same thing."

"And who is Brianna Walsh?" Clare asks, her eyes twinkling.

"The president of the VR company."

Those blue eyes.

"I think VR would be great for educational purposes," Ryan says. "I have an app to create virtual house plans. You can walk inside the finished house before you even lay the foundation."

"Hey, Mom, can I go play in my room?"

"Sure, Izzy."

"Make sure you say bye to me before you leave, Aunt Ren," Izzy calls as she turns down the hall to her bedroom.

"Will do, kiddo." I rest my head back on the couch and take a deep breath.

"You okay?" Clare asks.

"Yeah," I say with a sigh.

"Can I ask why I saw tears in your eyes before?"

I lean forward, my elbows on my knees, and run my hands through my hair. "I had another nightmare earlier in the week."

"You know we haven't seen each other for a while, but I thought you said the last time we talked that the dreams stopped. What's going on, Ren? It will be three years in a few months."

I move to the French doors. The sun is setting, displaying a red, orange, and yellow sky. The colors of flames. My right hand caresses the ragged scars through my blouse. "Yeah...I know."

CHAPTER EIGHT

Another restless night.

My eyes flash open. My breathing is heavy. I comb my fingers through my damp hair. The bedsheets are nowhere to be found, except for a corner tangled around my foot.

I walk to the bathroom and rest my hands on the basin. Dark circles stare back at me in the mirror. "You look like you've aged ten years," I tell myself. I need to get myself together for the VR presentation at school today.

After a shower and lots of makeup, I reexamine myself in the full-length mirror on the closet door. I'm wearing my long-sleeved, cobalt-blue dress with a white scarf, black belt, and black flats. At least I still have my hourglass body, even though it's becoming a little saggy in the middle. "Not bad after going ten rounds with a bedsheet," I tell my reflection.

As I open the door leading to the garage, my phone rings. "Hello?"

"Good morning, beautiful."

I stop in my tracks, the door halfway open. "Who is this?"

A male voice says matter-of-factly, "Someone who is admiring you from afar."

My blood runs cold. I have no idea who this could be. "Please don't call me again."

"You need someone to take care of you and your injury. I'm that person."

My eyes dart around the room. I peer out the front window in the dining room. My heartbeat accelerates.

"I don't need anyone to take care of me. Please do not call me again." I hit the *end call* button.

What the hell was that? And who was that? Maybe I need to block this number. If I only knew how.

CHAPTER NINE

Bri stands at the entrance to my office. "You looked deep in thought. I didn't want to startle you."

"No, please come in."

"Everyone ready for the demonstration?" Bri asks.

"Yes, they're assembled in the gym."

"Well, let's not keep them waiting." She steps aside and touches my left elbow, guiding me through the door. Without thinking, I pull my arm back into my body.

I wonder if she notices.

Her touch is gentle and tender.

The rest of her team stands in the hall, each holding multiple boxes.

Bri walks beside me. She is about three inches taller than my five foot six. She strides with energy and self-assurance, leaving no doubt about the ability of her team or herself.

As we walk, she asks, "Would you like to go—uh—never mind."

I stop. Did she…?

Bri takes two steps ahead of me before she realizes I'm not with her and turns. "Did I say something wrong?"

"No." I catch up to her. I hear her sigh.

In the gym, the teachers stand in three small groups, talking animatedly.

"Good afternoon. Thank you for joining us today. I appreciate you taking the time to be here," I say. "I want to introduce you to the virtual reality team by JAWS. They'll be demonstrating their VR programs."

The history department head, Melissa, says, "I did some research, and I'm excited to learn how this VR works. That's what they call it, right? I hear it can benefit our students."

Bri responds, "That's one of the reasons we're here today. The other reason is to demonstrate the ingenuity, adaptability, and flexibility"—she looks at me and winks—"of VR and how it can be a real-world language."

I flush.

Sarah takes a step forward, holding two black boxes, and says, "We have headsets and wands for all of you. And we've programmed each with specific apps related to your area of study."

"Let me introduce Jared and Anthony, our app developers," Bri adds, "Guys, will you please distribute the headsets and start the demonstrations?"

"You mean we have our own headsets?" asks math teacher Randy.

"Yes. We will demonstrate how to use them, and then you can take them home and play around with them for a week or two."

"Then we will all meet again and discuss your experiences and share if we think VR can enhance our students' educational experience," Darlene adds.

"Okay, let's rock and roll," Jared says.

The teachers approach Sarah, Jared, and Anthony to be fitted out with the headsets. Soon, they're spaced out accordingly, so they don't run into each other during the demonstration.

"They look as silly as I felt the other day," I say, chuckling.

"Yeah. Oh, by the way, speaking of people and how they look—your dress. That color suits you."

She noticed.

"O-oh. Thank you." I feel my heartbeat in my ear.

"Earlier, I was—earlier, I—would you like to have dinner with me after the presentation?"

I freeze, my heartbeat getting louder. How do I answer her? Do I want to go to dinner with her? Am I ready? I look out the door and point down the hallway. "I, um—I have paperwork to finish in my office, and it will probably take me into the evening. So..."

"Oh, okay."

Is it just me, or does her face fall? "So"—I jerk a thumb toward the gym door—"I need to get back to my office."

"O-okay. So...I'll stop by your office after the demonstration is completed. If that's okay?"

"Yes. Please...do." I gaze squarely into her eyes, which are locked on mine. "I—I'd...like to see you...know how it went."

God, first I tell her I don't want to have dinner with her, then I'm stuttering about wanting to see her after the presentation. Get a grip, Renata.

"No problem. I'll stop by," she says, turning to the group.

She stirs something in me—a tingle I wasn't sure I could ever feel again.

* * *

About an hour later, footsteps clamor in the hallway, coming toward my office. Bri is talking, her voice deep and robust like bourbon. Everyone laughs.

"Come in. How did the demonstration go?"

"It went well. The staff is very excited," Darlene says.

"And they caught on fast," Anthony adds.

"We'll meet again in two weeks and collect their feedback," Darlene says.

"Would you guys mind staying a few minutes? Darlene, can you stay too?" I ask.

"Sure, no problem," Sarah says.

I turn to Bri, with her penetrating blue eyes. She nods.

"I'm assuming you're anticipating the cost may be prohibitive for public schools," she says as I take my seat behind my desk. Anthony and Jared say their goodbyes and head out.

"It has crossed my mind."

"Not to worry. I have a foundation that gives grants for educational VR projects." Just then, her phone rings. She looks at the screen, takes a deep breath, and releases it. Then, she presses a button and says, "Sorry, where were we?"

"Your foundation—it sounds like your company has thought of everything," I say.

"My foundation isn't connected with the company, but I did start it from my share of the profits so I can give back to the community."

Sarah jumps in. "Bri's foundation supports LGBTQ equality, housing equity, women's and human rights, water accessibility... just to mention a few."

"Do you offer this opportunity to all of your potential clients?"

"Most, but not all."

"So why us?"

"You're one of the first high schools in this part of the state to show an interest in VR," Bri says. "We don't want the cost to stop you from having the opportunity. If it's a success here, then the notion will spread." Her phone rings again. She glances at her phone and says, "Sorry, I need to take this."

"Please go ahead."

She answers, "Liz. I'm at an appointment. Can this wait?"

A pause. She holds up a finger to wait and walks into the hallway.

Who's Liz? Maybe she's the woman Bri had dinner with the other week when I wished it could have been me.

"While we wait, can you tell me where the bathroom is?" Sarah asks.

"Sure, I can show you," Darlene offers.

A minute later, Bri returns and says, "Sorry again."

"Everything okay?"

"I hope so." She takes a deep breath. "Okay, so…we were talking about you being one of the first high schools in the area. And the grant opportunity."

"Yes. So if we use VR, you would use us in your marketing to other potential schools?"

"Yes—with your permission, of course. This is a business. However, we really do believe in the utility of VR in education. We don't want the cost to impede a school's opportunity to access it."

"So, you're not just giving us—me—this grant opportunity because I refuse to go out with you?"

Bri's mouth opens. Nothing comes out.

I could hear a pin drop.

"Nooo." She tilts her head and, with a half grin, continues, "The foundation is built on integrity and honesty. And I don't give up that easily."

My stomach drops. "Well—" Way to go, Renata, jumping to conclusions as usual.

"My intention behind asking you out was me wanting to know you better," she says stiffly. "I find you attractive, and from observing you with your staff, who obviously admire you, and from all your accomplishments"—she motions to the plaques on the wall—"I think you're a kind, caring, and passionate person."

Sarah and Darlene walk back into the office but stop abruptly, their heads swiveling between Bri and me. Silence engulfs the room.

Finally, Bri says, "I have some family business I need to address so Darlene can you be the contact person for this project and liaise with Sarah?"

"Sure, no problem."

"Great."

"Bri. Wait." I take a step toward her and touch her arm. My sleeve moves up when I touch her, revealing the scars.

She stares at my hand and retracts her arm. "Sarah will keep me informed." And smiling, says, "And I hope to see you again, Ms. Santos."

"Have a good evening, Ms. Walsh."

"Darlene, thanks for initiating the contact with JAWS, and I look forward to hopefully working with you all on this project."

Bri turns and walks out the door.

CHAPTER TEN

The next day, I drive into work, reliving my conversation with Bri. She told me she found me attractive. Did she not notice the scar on my hand? Is that why she pulled her arm away?

My phone rings. A male voice comes across the car speakers. "Good morning, beautiful."

I glance at the screen. Unknown caller. "Stop calling me, whoever you are."

"I'm an admirer. I want to take care of you."

My mouth drops, my heart racing. I hit the *end call* button. I need to find someone who can show me how to block this caller.

I'm sitting at my office desk, and there's a knock on my door. "Hey, Renata, you here?" Darlene asks.

"No! I'm on a beach in California, sipping a margarita."

"Wow, you in a bad mood?"

"Sorry. What's up?"

"Just wondered if you want to add any other items to the staff meeting agenda for the—then the truck backs up and runs over me."

"What? A truck?"

"Where is your head?"

I heave a long breath. "I got an anonymous call this morning from a man who said he is admiring me from afar and wants to take care of me."

Darlene's jaw drops. "No way."

"Yes way. It's freaking me out."

"You need to contact the police."

I nod. "I will."

"Are you sure you will? This sounds creepy."

"Look, if it happens again…"

Darlene gives me a look. "Renata, come on. Did you ever think about how he knows your phone number?"

"Okay, okay, okay." I hadn't thought of that. "Now, can we move on?"

"I'm serious."

"I got your message."

"At least block his call."

"I don't know how to do that."

Darlene retrieves my phone off my desk, asks for my passcode and pushes a few buttons. "It's blocked. He can still leave a message, but you won't have to answer his call."

"Thanks."

Darlene takes a deep breath and clears her throat. "I…am…wondering if you want to share what happened yesterday between you and Bri—um, Ms. Walsh?"

"She asked me out."

She takes a step toward me. "So? What's wrong with her asking you out? Isn't that what you wanted?"

"I accused her of giving us the grant opportunity because I wouldn't go out with her."

She stops in her tracks. "You what?"

"I know. I know. I have no idea where that came from. It was…immature, rude, and unprofessional." I turn away to hide the tears beginning to build.

"Ren. It's nearly three years. I cannot imagine the strength and courage you had to get through what you did. But—"

"But?" My voice rises as I point from my neck to my hip. "You. Don't. See. The. Scars."

"I've seen your hand, ear, and neck, even though you try to hide it."

"Of course, I hide it!" I pace back and forth in front of my office window.

"Ren, no one here ever mentions your scars. All I hear is how much they admire you—before *and* after this. You came back to work after six months and it was like you never left. You were the same supportive, energetic, inspiring leader."

If she only knew how hard it was to come back. But I did.

"Well, I'm their boss. I pretty much dictate their careers."

"You don't believe that." She stands beside me, placing her hand on my left shoulder.

I jerk out from under her hand, but she replaces it.

"Ren. You need to start letting people touch you."

"You're touching me."

"Yes. Right. This is the first time you've let my hand rest on your shoulder. But I mean emotionally, not just physically."

I take a deep breath. A tear escapes down my cheek.

"Remember when I started working with you all those years ago and how we'd travel to Columbus to the professional lesbian social group?"

"Yeah."

"Dances and dinners. We had so much fun. That's where I met Nancy."

"How can I forget? You didn't stop talking about her for weeks."

"I know—until you finally threatened to call her yourself for me if I didn't."

"And when you finally called her, she said yes."

Darlene shakes her head and says, "Yeah, and that lasted eight months."

I chuckle. "Yeah, Nancy was kind of weird. Sorry."

"And remember sitting on your patio discussing how to improve student scores?"

"Yeah, I remember."

"What *I* remember about those times was your spark for adventure and excitement." Darlene squeezes my shoulder. "But since the fire, the sparkle has gone."

I sidestep her, and her hand falls off my shoulder. "It went up in flames, along with thirty percent of my body."

We stand there for a few seconds before the administrative secretary, Mrs. Wilson, knocks on the doorjamb. "Ms. Santos, sorry to interrupt, but Ms. Thomas is expecting a parent for a disciplinary issue and would like to talk with you before she meets with them."

I wipe my tears away and brace myself to help the assistant principal. "Tell her I'll be right there. Thank you for relaying the message."

Darlene reaches for my shoulder again. "I don't know how to get the spark back."

CHAPTER ELEVEN

The following week, nothing unusual happens at school—which is just as well because my concentration keeps being interrupted by thoughts of Bri and my absurd and inappropriate reaction to her asking me out.

The echo of the bell reverberates off the walls, and Darlene and I take our positions in the hall. We are responsible for crowd control as students exit their classrooms, some spilling out into the hallway while others talk with friends, they haven't seen all day. The air is filled with hugs, laughter, and enthused chatter as everyone heads to their next class.

As a tall student walks by us, I say, "Mr. Boyd, outstanding tackle on Friday." I raise and reach above my head as far as I can. He slaps my hand.

"Thanks, Ms. Santos." His smile dimples and he continues to walk to class.

The second bell rings, and last-minute stragglers enter classrooms as we walk back to our offices.

As we turn down the hall, Darlene says, "Uh…Sarah Reynolds called. She and Bri want a meeting with us."

I stop and stare at her. "She asked to meet with both of us?"

"Yes."

"Did Sarah say why she wanted the meeting?"

"No. Not specifically."

"Okay." I thought Bri would never want to talk or see me again.

"So, if Brianna Walsh asks you out again, what are you going to do?" Darlene asks.

"I think I squelched that topic, don't you?"

"Who knows? Suppose she doesn't ask you. You could ask her?" We turn down the administration hallway. "Here's my stop. Think about it. What would it hurt?"

I pass my office door and go out a door leading to the parking lot. The sun peeks around a dark cloud, the air chilly with the close of fall. I think back to my last few conversations with Darlene. Is she right? Have I built an emotional wall around myself?

Ask Brianna to go on a date? What could it hurt?

My mind makes a mental list of reasons why I shouldn't, starting with reliving the pain of Maggie's rejection, to having to explain the scars, not to mention my fear of being touched. Yet I ache for human contact.

I stop by Darlene's office and say, "I guess we need to schedule that meeting."

"How about next week? Tuesday at four?"

I mentally search my calendar. "I think that will work for me. Will you call and schedule it?"

"Sure."

Mrs. Wilson stops at Darlene's office, holding a bouquet of red long-stemmed roses. "Ms. Santos, these are for you."

"For me?" I ask with surprise. "They are gorgeous."

The secretary hands them to me. I inhale deeply. The fragrance is soothing.

"Thank you. Who would send these?" I ask Darlene.

"Is there a card?"

I push the roses aside and find the card. "Yes."

"Well, what does it say?"

"It says, 'Looking forward to seeing you again.'"

"Is there a signature?"

"No."

"Someone sends you flowers, and they don't sign the card? Don't you think that's odd?"

"Very." Unease replaces my initial surprise.

"Or"—Darlene taps her mouth with her fingers—"romantic? Maybe Bri is a romantic and not giving up, and she wants to soften you up."

"Like Shelly?" I ask to take the focus off me. Could it really have been Bri?

Darlene blushes. "Oh, stop. She sent me flowers for Christmas."

"Yeah, then there were flowers on your birthday—"

She smiles. "Yeah, I never knew she had a crush on me in college, and it's lasted this long."

"So, is it getting serious?"

"She's in Florida and I'm here. But she can work from anywhere, so we've been talking and Zooming. But we're not talking about me, we're talking about you. Could the flowers be from Bri?"

"Like I said, I acted…well, you know." The flowers could be from her. Do I want them to be from her?

"Well, who else would it be?"

I can't remember the last time my heart has felt this hopeful.

CHAPTER TWELVE

"Is the conference room ready for the meeting with JAWS?"
I ask Mrs. Wilson as I pass her desk.

"Yes, Ms. Santos. All set up. I've put water bottles and the
cookies you brought this morning on the table."

"Thank you so much. You take excellent care of me."

"Well, you take care of all of us. By the way, those Portuguese
cookies are delicious."

I remember how anxious I was last night, making the spikes-
of-corn cookies for the meeting. When I opened the oven door,
the heat had rushed out and hit my face and arms, and my whole
body tensed. But I stood up straight, took a deep breath, and
exhaled, telling myself, *I can do this.*

And I did.

"When our guests arrive, will you please bring them to the
conference room?"

"Ms. Santos."

I stop and turn. Bri.

"Ms. Walsh." I move to her and extend my unscarred hand. "I'm glad to see you again." I hope she hears my sincerity.

"Ms. Santos—" she says, her face impassive.

"Please call me Renata."

"That's personal. You don't want to keep it professional?"

I guess I deserve that.

"Ms. Walsh, can we talk after our meeting?"

She glances at her watch. "I have another meeting after this one. If time allows, yes, I can stay." She moves past me without making eye contact and takes a seat.

Sarah and Darlene enter, chatting amicably.

"Sarah, good to see you again," I say feebly. "Please sit anywhere you'd like. Would you like some water?"

Darlene touches Sarah's arm. "Try the cookies. Renata made them."

I pick up the tray and offer them both a cookie.

Bri takes one and slowly bites into it. "Mmm!" Her lips are covered in crumbs as she asks, "What are they?"

Darlene tilts her head at me.

"Oh, sorry, they're espigas de milho, Portuguese spikes-of-corn cookies," I answer.

"Can I have another?" Sarah asks. "They are *delicious*."

I move the tray toward Sarah. "Have as many as you want."

Sarah grabs two.

"I would like another Portuguese spiked worm, if I may." Bri smiles, showing crumbs on her top lip.

I gesture to my top lip with my finger.

She opens her mouth, and her tongue darts out to lick the crumbs off her lip. Then, she moves her tongue slowly over her top lip.

My stomach flips.

I turn to Darlene, whose eyes move back and forth between us, and clear my throat. "Okay. Let's get started." I sit next to Darlene. Bri and Sarah sit across the table. I nod to Bri, who nods back. "From what I've heard, the staff is having fun with it."

"They will be meeting as a group to organize their feedback," Darlene adds.

"Well, let me tell you the reason we're here." Bri takes a deep breath. "Our company is in the process of being acquired by another VR company."

I sit up straight in my chair. "What?"

"No need to worry. Our terms include keeping all of our employees. I'll stay on as president until I retire in three years, then I'll sit on the board, along with two of our employees."

"No existing employees from either company will be furloughed," Sarah adds.

"Jared and Anthony will remain as directors of programming, and Sarah will become vice president, so when I retire, she will take over as president," Bri explains.

I say nothing. Will I see her again?

Darlene asks, "Will we continue to work with you, Jared, and Anthony?"

"Yes. You are stuck with us," Sarah jokes.

"Then I have no concerns," Darlene responds.

Bri turns to me. "Do you have any, Ms. Santos?"

I lean back into my chair. My breathing slows. "No, not as long as we continue to work with…you…and your staff."

"I want you both to know that this will not impact our working relationship in any way," Bri says.

"Is there anything else?" Darlene asks. "If not, I'd like to share with Sarah the ideas the teachers forwarded to me."

"Great."

Darlene motions for Sarah to follow her. "Let's go to my office."

Bri pauses as the two leave. "I need to talk with Ms. Santos. I'll stop by your office when I'm ready to head out, Darlene."

Silence.

Finally, Bri stands. "So. You wanted to talk with me?"

"Yes." I fold my hands into my lap and hope for the best.

I roll my shoulders and say, "I want to apologize for what I said when we last spoke. It was wrong, and I'm sorry."

Bri sits down. "Why did you assume I was—what, bribing you to go out with me?"

I wince. "I thought you were taking pity on me—us, the school. We are not the richest school district."

"Take pity on you? No. Why would I do such a thing? My foundation believes in public education, so we give grants to schools for a variety of projects, not just VR."

"Again"—I search her eyes—"I'm sorry for making the wrong assumption."

She tilts her head. "Apology accepted."

"And I want to thank you for the roses."

"Roses? What roses?"

"Ah. Wrong assumption again." I walk toward the door. "Um—I thought—I thought you sent them to me. There was no signature on the card." My face grows warm, probably turning as red as the roses.

She comes up beside me, rubbing my forearm. Does she feel the scars?

"Ms. Santos, if I were to send you flowers, I would first find out your favorite color and make sure the card said they were from me."

"Good to know," I say hoarsely, opening the door.

Bri nudges me as we walk. "By the way, what color rose is your favorite?"

Our shoulders touch. "Yellow."

Bri smiles, and we walk to my office in silence.

I stop a few steps from Darlene's office. Bri stops and stares at me, waiting for me to say something.

Can I do this? Do I want to do this? My heart starts to race, and my breath shortens.

"Renata, you okay?" she asks in a soft-spoken voice.

God, I'm fifty-eight years old. You would think it wouldn't be this hard to ask someone out for dinner.

I take a deep breath. "Just a minute." Deep breath in, deep breath out.

"Renata?"

I can do this. I inhale and say as fast as I can, "I want to ask if you would like to get something to eat?"

I did it. I exhale.

Bri angles her head. A smile grows until dimples appear, and her blue eyes light up as she says, "You mean now?"

"Yeah." I smile, "I'm caught up with all of my paperwork."

"I would love to."

I touch her arm. "Great. There's a Mexican restaurant right down the road. El Cazador."

"Yeah, I know it."

"I'll meet you there in fifteen minutes."

My body suddenly feels different. Less tense. I'm unsure if it's the adrenaline or how she looked at me when she said yes.

CHAPTER THIRTEEN

I gather my belongings from my office and ask myself as I walk to my car, *What have I done?* Nothing I can do now. Stay calm. It's only meeting for dinner. It's not a date. Is it?

I walk into the restaurant and see Bri sitting in a booth on the left side by the windows. She smiles and waves.

"Thanks for agreeing to have dinner with me." I sit and nervously unravel the utensils from the napkin and place the napkin on my lap. Then I grab and peruse the menu.

The server approaches the table and asks us about drinks.

"Coke for me," I say.

"Same, for me."

Bri asks about the menu items as she reviews her choices. I tell her everything is very tasty.

The server brings our drinks, and we place our order.

I gaze out the window and watch a family of four walking toward the door and I tell myself, *say something, you asked her here.*

I turn to Bri across from me, where she sits upright, her hands crossed on top of the table her smile still on her face. "So…ah…tell me how you got involved with virtual reality?"

Bri's enthusiasm surfaces as she speaks, her blue eyes brightening with every word. She had initially started out as a therapist dedicated to helping families affected by mental health issues, substance abuse, and disabilities. When the opportunity arose years later to join a university program that conducted research in the same fields, Bri was ecstatic. Without hesitation, she accepted the invitation.

"And that's where you met your partners?"

"Yeah. We worked together for ten years, I think," she chuckles. "Time flies when you're having fun."

She is interrupted when our food is delivered.

The buzz of surrounding conversations disappears and I'm only focused on Bri as she explains that she and her team had been experimenting with virtual reality to understand its inner workings before they started looking for grants. Ideas such as pinpointing triggers that lead alcoholics to drink and creating an interactive experience of what it's like to be hard of hearing had come up in their discussions.

"How do you do that?"

She gives the example of creating the environment of a bar, and the person would put on the headset and be in the bar. Then the therapist guides the person to identify their feelings, cravings, and triggers that could tempt them to have a drink and work on developing strategies to counteract those temptations.

"Wow. That sounds intense."

"It could be."

"Interesting."

"But we never got the opportunity to take our ideas to the next level as we couldn't get funding."

"That's too bad."

"Then, one day at lunch, we jokingly talked about starting our own VR company. The four of us were tired of working under the constraints of a university environment and not making much money, we said to each other, let's do it. And we did."

"That was very ambitious of you all and very risky."

"Yeah, and a lot of fun once the legal aspects were ironed out."

"Tell me this, I'm curious. How did being a therapist and researching how VR can help alcoholics lead to starting your own VR company in the education field?"

"JAWS started with a VR project for a medical school. We took our original ideas about what it's like to be in a wheelchair. We created a grocery store where the person is in a wheelchair, and you must wheel yourself around the store and shop for groceries."

"So, the person learns the life challenges of a person in a wheelchair."

"Right."

"Then we created an environment where the med student was in a doctor's office with a person who is hard of hearing except the med student is the hard of hearing patient."

"Interesting."

"The medical school was so impressed with our applications that they asked if we could develop a virtual environment for their anatomy and surgery classes."

"That was the opportunity you needed."

"Yes. And that led us to other educational applications, some of which we demonstrated with your staff."

"Quite a journey."

"Yeah. So what about you?" Bri asks as she takes a bite of her fajitas.

"Oh." I use my napkin and wipe my mouth as Bri stares intently at me.

"I always wanted to be a teacher from when I was very young. I use to play teacher all the time with my younger sister. Clare."

"Oh, you have a sister."

"Yes, she is married to Ryan."

Bri interrupts, "Ryan, the brother-in-law with a VR set."

"Yes, and they have a daughter, my niece, Izzy."

"How old is Izzy?"

"Ten."

I go on to explain my career path from science teacher to getting my administrator's certificate to become assistant principal and then principal.

"Sounds like a lot of studying to me."

"It was, but worth it. I enjoy working with young people and the teachers."

We both sip our soda and our eyes meet over the top of our glasses. Bri lowers her glass and says, "Thanks for inviting me to dinner."

I smile. "Thanks for accepting. After how I turned you down and the flower assumption, I wasn't sure what you would do."

"I'd never turn down a dinner invitation from a beautiful woman."

My face heats up from embarrassment. "You must get a lot of invitations for dinner from women?"

"No." A blush moves up her neck. "You're the first in a long time."

My heart is beating like a bass drum. "Do you have any siblings?"

Bri inhales. "Yes, a brother, younger. His name is David."

She goes on and tells me he lives in Cincinnati, is married, they see each other about twice a month and talk on the phone regularly.

Suddenly I get a chill. I gaze around the room.

"Something wrong?" Bri asks with concern on her face.

"No. Just got a chill. A weird feeling like someone is watching me."

Bri laughs softly. "I'm watching you."

Again, my face burns with embarrassment.

We laugh and talk for another hour or so, share phone numbers, and Bri agrees to call me soon. A sense of warmth washes over me. I think back to the last few weeks with Maggie—the dulled conversations, the dinners when we barely said two words to each other, the way even a simple hug felt like an effort. I should have recognized that our relationship had been damaged long before the fire.

CHAPTER FOURTEEN

I throw my coat over the breakfast nook chair and my briefcase onto the kitchen counter. After rummaging through my briefcase past pens, papers, keys, and dirty Kleenex, finally, at the bottom, I find my phone and call Clare.

"Hey, sis."

"Hi, Clare."

"Are you calling to cancel Sunday dinner?"

I pace in circles around my kitchen. "Um…no." My voice quivers.

"Something wrong? Your voice sounds—are you okay?"

"Yes, yes." I pause.

"Ren?"

On my second circle through my house, I blurt out, "I invited Bri to dinner with me after work today."

"Bri? You mean Brianna Walsh?"

"Yes. Her."

"You don't sound convinced it was a good idea."

Silence.

"Sis, you still there?"

"Clare, I'm terrified."

My heart pounds, and my legs tremble. I place my hand on the wooden framework of the bay window to steady myself.

"Ren. Take deep breaths. Slowly inhale through your nose and exhale through your mouth."

I do as she says. A few times and my breathing returns to normal. "This is the second time I've fought off an anxiety attack in two days." I walk into the living room and plop down in my favorite leather chair, throwing my legs over one flared arm and leaning back against the other. "Thanks for talking me through it."

"I love you, Renata."

"I know."

"So how did it go?"

"I was nervous in the beginning but then, after we started to talk, it felt...good."

"That's wonderful, Ren."

"But when I walked in the door, I'm back to feeling scared."

"Scared of what?"

"I'm opening myself up to be...to be..."

"To be rejected again?"

"Yes." I sit upright in the chair and run my hand over my face. "Once she sees me—all of me—she's gonna run for the hills."

"Stop. You don't know that."

"Why wouldn't she?" I leap out of the chair and walk into the dining room. "No one has held or touched me since..."

"Ren. Ren."

"What if—"

"Ren. Stop. Listen to me." Clare's voice goes up an octave.

"You don't see my body, Clare. No one has."

"I've seen the scars from your neck and down your arm."

"But not the rest. They're not—it isn't pretty—it's—"

Clare's voice goes up another octave. "Renata! Stop!"

"Okay." I take a deep breath. "I'm listening."

"You had dinner. Was it even a date? You're way ahead of yourself. No one is taking their clothes off."

I turn to look out the window. "Okay."

"Take it slow, honey. There is no rush."

"You don't understand. I'm attracted to her, and—"

Clare interrupts, "You can go slow."

"I never thought I'd be attracted to anyone again."

"Remember the peer support chat we did with the Phoenix Society? What was one of the most important things we learned?"

"To communicate." I sigh. "And practice authenticity."

"And authenticity means?"

"Is this a test?"

Clare chuckles. "Yes."

"To be honest with yourself and with others."

"Correct."

I smile in spite of myself. "Is the test over?"

"Yes, you passed. Back to Bri. She must have impressed you, or you wouldn't want to take this risk."

"She did. She's confident, smart, forgiving"—I chuckle to myself—"and she sends out this aura of calmness."

"I know this is a big step for you, but just remember: go slow and talk."

"Right." I pause. "Go slow and talk. Got it. Thanks, sis. See you around two thirty on Sunday."

"Great. Be ready for the touch football game."

"Can I bring anything?"

"Just you. And Ren, take it slow."

CHAPTER FIFTEEN

Looking at my reflection in the long mirror, I'm torn between accepting Bri's invitation to see the wooden troll sculptures at Aullwood Audubon Center and Farm or staying home. I had read about the enormous trolls throughout the farm and heard some students enthusiastically talking about it. With no other plans for this Saturday, why does the idea of going frighten me so much?

It's been a challenging, heartbreaking almost-three years.

Clare and Ryan almost lost their daughter in a fire and did lose their house. I was severely burnt. Izzy believed that was her fault because I helped her get out of the house first. Over the long months of recovery, nurses came to my house to change my arm, back, and hip dressings. I attended weekly physical and occupational therapy sessions and outpatient rehabilitation. I wore compression garments over my burns and grafts when I could tolerate the fabric against my skin. I attended family therapy with Izzy, Clare, and Ryan—*and* individual therapy. And then overarching all of that was the pain…

And Maggie left me.

I hid the scars and became a hermit, even after I had returned to work. I occasionally went to Clare's for Sunday dinner—and even then, I skipped quite a few. I continued to go to work, just going through the motions. A few friends continued to call and ask me to join them, but I always declined. I don't blame them for not staying in touch.

But it's up to me to rejoin the living. I'm tired of being alone.

I take a deep breath. Looking back, I may be stronger than I think.

I focused all my time on my recovery. My recovery from what? Look at me. My nightmares and my body continue to remind me of pain, loss, and isolation.

I acknowledge the woman looking back at me in the mirror. Everything matches: my red sweatshirt over my white turtleneck, my jeans, my red-and-white Hoka sneakers. I'm ready for a walk with the trolls.

I raise my arms out toward the mirror like I'm gonna hug myself, but I shrug instead. "What the hell. Too late now."

* * *

The doorbell rings. I take a deep breath and open the door. There's Bri, a smile and a twinkle in her eye. "Ready?"

"Yes." *Ready as I'll ever be*, I say to myself.

"This is going to be fun," Bri says as she opens the car door for me. Then she skips around to the driver's side and jumps in.

She touches my arm. "I'm happy to see you again."

We hum along to the radio and chat about our week as we drive to the farm. I share stories of my budget woes threatening to cut staff and Bri shares her excitement about a new app being developed for a history class.

We pay our entrance fee, grab brochures, and off we go to find the trolls.

I read out loud as we walk on the dirt and wood-chip trail, trees on either side. "There are three giant trolls nestled in the woods. The exhibit is permanent and one of only nine in the United States. There are three trolls—Bo, Bodil, and Bibbi."

I watch Bri intently as she walks ahead of me, her nose buried in the brochure. She steps with a sort of giddy determination, like an intrepid explorer, totally engrossed in her mission. I quicken my pace to catch up and grab her arm just before she walks straight into a gnarled tree limb that hung low over the trail. Bri yelps in surprise and glances up at me before quickly averting her gaze to the hanging branch above us.

"Thanks."

She grabs my hand and pulls me forward. "Come on." As we continue walking, she doesn't let go of my hand. And I don't want her to.

The cloudy skies overhead with a slight breeze make me glad I brought my sweater vest to put over my sweatshirt. Bri's copper-brown L.L.Bean utility jacket hugs her hips. The hips that bump into mine as we walk hand in hand. Birds chirp and squirrels chatter as they run up and down the trees.

At the same time, we both spot one of the trolls standing in an open space surrounded by bare trees and thigh-high field grass. I grab the brochure from her hand. "Hey." I point and say, "That's Bibbi."

"How tall is it?"

"The brochure says seventeen feet."

We walk to Bibbi and admire the sculpture made from recycled materials such as discarded dollar-store shelves, old pallets, shipping materials, large metal canisters, and fallen trees.

"This is amazing," I say as I walk around Bibbi. Bri joins me, and we inspect the sculpture.

"Let me take your picture," Bri says as she pulls out her phone.

I stand in front of it and spread my arms out to my side, like a bird, just like Bibbi.

I jog to Bri and look at the picture. I smile. And Bri says, "You look great. And it looks like Bibbi is chasing you." We both laugh.

A family of three walks up to Bibbi and I ask if they will take our picture. I hand them my phone. We put our arms around each other and lean our heads together. Bri grabs my hand, and we continue our search of Bo and Bodil.

CHAPTER SIXTEEN

After our successful hunt for the trolls, we decide to celebrate with a meal at TJ Chumps. We sit in a U-shaped booth and order food and drinks. We take turns going through the photos we'd snapped of our adventure.

Bri swipes right and says, "Look at this one."

I scoot close enough that our thighs touch. "It looks like Bibbi is stepping on you." We both laugh.

TJ Chumps has three TVs hanging from each wall, broadcasting a variety of football and soccer games. The volume is turned down and the only sound is that of patron's conversations and cheers.

Bri looks up when a man in an Ohio State University sweatshirt yells, "Touchdown" and raises his fist in the air as he says, "O...H." And the other patrons, including Bri and I, say, "I...O."

I grab my phone. "Look at this one."

Bri moves closer and lays her arm on the back of the booth behind me.

My phone dings, signaling a voice mail message.

"What was that?"

"A voice mail message."

"You want to check who it is?"

"Not now." As I know, I've only blocked one phone number. "I'll listen to it later."

I swipe my phone with my left hand, and the next picture shows both of us kneeling in front of Bodil. In the picture, I notice Bri staring at me, her arm holding me close. Suddenly I remember how safe I felt at that moment.

My thoughts are interrupted when the server brings our food. We dig in to our hamburgers and fries.

"All that walking," I say between bites, "made me hungry."

I observe Bri gaze up at the OSU game and then back to take a bite of her burger. Then glances at me, and a smile appears. Her eyes are not searching or distracted. They are direct and gentle, yet simultaneously penetrating and intense. I want to grab her hand or reach out and touch her face.

Another yell of "O...H...I...O."

"That was the best hamburger I've had in a long time," I say.

"Glad you like it."

"I did and"—I lay my hand on Bri's—"I'm glad you asked me to see the trolls."

Bri covers my hand with hers and gazes downward as she tenderly caresses my knuckles with her thumb.

When I realize it's my left hand with the scars I instantly pull my hand from hers and place it on my lap.

Bri looks up with confusion written all over her face. "Did I do something wrong?"

"No. I'm tired and..."

"Was that a scar on your hand?"

"Ah..." I slide away from Bri. "Yeah. No big deal."

"How did you get..."

Bri's phone rings, and David's name pops up on the screen. She looks at it and then at me. I nod.

"David, what's up?"

Bri moves to the side of the booth. I turn my head to watch the game, trying not to overhear.

The one thing I do hear is the word *sponsor*.

Bri places her phone on the table and looks troubled.

"Everything okay?"

"Yeah." Bri runs her fingers through her hair and then rubs her eyes.

"If you need to talk…"

"He's a recovering alcoholic. Been sober for five years for about the fourth time. Five years seems to be his nemesis. Anyway, he's up for a big promotion. He's worked so hard, this time, to get his life back on the right track, and he's feeling stressed."

"So you told him to contact his sponsor? Sorry, I wasn't trying to eavesdrop."

Bri waves her hands. "No worries. Yes, I did, and he said he would."

I rub her shoulder. "Well, that's a good thing, right?"

"Yeah. Yeah." Bri straightens up. "So, your hand?"

I move away from Bri. "I've had a wonderful day with you, Bri. This is the most exercise and laughing I've done in a long time. But hiking has made me tired. So, if you don't mind, I believe I'm ready to head home."

"Sure, let me get the check and pay."

"No, let me."

We lock eyes, and each of us tries to make our case for who will cover the bill. Finally, Bri breaks our gaze and says she'd get this one, and I could get the next one.

I feel my cheeks heat up as I smile, and a flutter in my heart at the thought of a next time.

CHAPTER SEVENTEEN

The quick ride to my house is too short, and I wish I lived farther so I could spend more time with Bri. As we pull into the driveway, Bri says, "I had a great time today. Can we get together again?"

I lay my hand on her arm. "I'd like that."

We discuss our upcoming week. Bri has to go out of town for a few days on business, so we agree to go out on Friday night.

"Maybe a movie and dinner?" asks Bri.

She asks me to pick a movie and a place to eat.

"I thought you were asking me out on a date? Shouldn't you be picking the movie and restaurant?"

Bri blushes and looks like she made a big faux pas. "Ah… yeah but I'm gonna be out of town…"

"You are so cute when you blush."

"Stop." She gets out of the car and opens my door. She walks me to the front door, and we stand, neither of us seemingly knowing what to say.

The soft rays of the porch light make Bri's eyes sparkle. I run my hands down Bri's arms and say, "Again, thanks for a wonderful day."

"You're welcome. I had a great time too."

We both hesitate.

Bri says, "I should be going. I'll call you later in the week to finalize our date."

Bri takes a hesitant step toward me. Her eyes soften as she extends her arms. I step into the embrace, her arms enveloping me in warmth. I return the hug with a slight squeeze.

As we separate, Bri says, "I'll call you on Thursday when I get back into town. Have a good week at work."

"You too," I say as she turns to walk back to her car.

She stops and turns. "Good night, Renata."

"Good night, Bri."

* * *

I'm sitting in my leather lounge chair, recalling the memories of my day with Bri. Her easy laughter, her playfulness, and how she had touched my hand so lightly still lingers. I can't believe that I had felt so comfortable around someone again. The hug we shared before parting was full of tenderness and warmth, but the truth I had kept from her weighs like a heavy stone on my chest. And then comes the familiar feeling of fear—why hadn't I told her about the fire? When should I tell her? Or even if I should tell her? It is an intense feeling of conflicting emotions, comfort and fear each fighting for dominance.

CHAPTER EIGHTEEN

The thought of Friday's date with Bri looms over me all week, a dark cloud threatening to rain down insecurities and doubt. But as Thursday arrives, so does her phone call. Her voice is a welcome relief from my anxious thoughts. I inform her that we will be dining at Olive Garden at five p.m., then taking in a movie—*Top Gun Maverick* or *Champions*. She chose the latter, seeing as she was the one who asked me on this date. As we chat further, Bri tells me about new schools interested in VR technology while I update her on our community meetings to garner support for the upcoming school levy.

I can hear the excitement in her voice when she talks about the infinite possibilities of VR, and I find myself caught up in it too.

As we speak, I can't help but marvel at how natural and easily our conversation flows. It's like we've known each other for years instead of just weeks. And before we know it, it's time to say goodbye.

As I push the *end call* button, I'm left feeling eager for Friday night to arrive. Maybe there's something more here than just a simple date. Maybe this is the start of something special if I can open myself to it.

Friday afternoon, I sit in my office reviewing my next week's schedule before heading home. I gather my things and head down the hall, my mind free to anticipate tonight's date with Bri.

I search for my phone in my satchel to see if Bri called. I have five messages. I listen to the first one from Clare. The second one is a male voice. "Hello, beautiful." I hit the *end call* button. The remaining three are from the same male caller. I throw my phone on the passenger seat and hit the steering wheel with the palms of my hands. "Please stop," I say to no one but myself.

I begin my drive home, and suddenly my phone rings again. My body tenses then relaxes when I see Bri's name on the screen on the dashboard. I hit the *answer* button. "Bri, it's you."

My muscles relax.

"Hey, Renata, you sound a little stressed. Everything okay?"

"Yeah. I'm looking forward to tonight."

"That's why I'm calling."

She's going to cancel. She saw the scar.

"I got a call from Liz…"

My heart stops beating. Liz, the same woman's name when she took a call in my office when we first met. "Liz? Who's Liz? Are you seeing another woman?"

Bri giggles. "No. No. Liz is David, my brother's, wife."

"Sorry. I…"

"No worries. Anyway, they're heading to Toledo to visit some college friends and wanted to stop on their way and have dinner with me."

My heart starts beating again. "Okay. We can have dinner another time."

"No, Renata, I'm not canceling. I wanted to know if it would be okay for them to join us for dinner?"

"Sure, that will be fine. I'll call and add two more to our reservation. And we can catch the movie after our early dinner."

"Great, I'll pick you up at four thirty. Thanks, Renata."

"I'll be ready. See you later."
"Oh, and by the way. I'm a one-woman woman."
I chuckle. "Good to know. Goodbye, Bri."

CHAPTER NINETEEN

The drive home from the movie allows me time to reflect on our evening. Dinner with David and Liz had gone well. David is an accountant, and Liz is a nurse. They live in Cincinnati. Bri and David's parents passed away when she was in her late thirties, her dad from a heart attack, and her mom from cancer. They both went to college and as David said, "Nothing out of the ordinary. I met Liz in college, and we traveled to Europe after graduation. We got jobs in different cities and decided to break up. Then about five years ago, we ran into each other again at a college friend's wedding."

Liz gazed at Bri who was looking at David.

Liz added, "Well, that's the short version."

David inhaled. "The long version is I struggled with alcohol in college. The only way Liz would go to Europe with me was if I stopped drinking."

"And you did," added Liz.

"But. But that German beer did me in, and we went our separate ways when we returned."

"I was married for twelve years then divorced." Liz continued, "Luckily, we had no children."

"I got married right after we broke up. Had two DUIs, and that marriage ended when I refused to admit I had a drinking problem."

I listened intently.

"I had multiple relationships that never worked out, and after my third DUI, Bri refused to bail me out, and I spent a year in jail."

Bri added, "That last time he was driving drunk, hit a tree, swerving to avoid hitting a child crossing the street. I told him he goes to inpatient treatment or I'm done with him."

David said, "And with the support of my wonderful wife and sister, Al-Anon and AA, I've been sober for five years since Liz and I got together again." Liz squeezed David's hand and Bri patted him on the back.

"And we married about four years ago."

"Congratulations," I said, "it takes a lot of courage to share that with someone you just met. Thank you."

There was a sigh of relief from everyone at the table.

I told them about Clare, Ryan, and Izzie but didn't mention the fire.

For the rest of dinner, there were family stories and laughter.

As Bri pulls into my driveway, she asks, "Did you like the movie?"

"Yes. I loved how the children taught the coach what was important in life and how to enjoy it again."

Bri turns to me, and grabs my hand. "I had a great time tonight."

"So did I. It was good to meet your brother and sister-in-law."

We walk to my front door and I ask if Bri would like to come in. She says she is still recuperating from her trip and could she take a rain check. I say of course.

We hug goodbye again only this time longer than usual. We both pull each other closer and I lean my head on Bri's shoulder, taking in the sweet smell of lavender. We step apart and Bri leans down and kisses my cheek.

I grab the door handle, turn and ask, "Since I met your family, how about this Sunday meeting mine?"

Bri raises her eyebrow. "Sure, I'd love to."

I step back and kiss her cheek. "I'll call you tomorrow with the time."

"Okay, looking forward to it. Good night, Renata."

"Good night, Bri."

CHAPTER TWENTY

After following Bri's directions, I turn into her driveway. It's a one-story brick ranch with a two-car garage on the left and a wraparound porch to the right. Tall oak and maple trees surround the house, almost bare now with the approaching winter.

Am I ready for this? I take a deep breath and knock.

Bri's grin cannot be contained. "Hi, you're right on time. Come in. Any problems with my directions?"

"Hi—no, not at all." I stand in the foyer. She is in a long-sleeved sweatshirt, a white mock turtleneck underneath. "I like your top."

"Thanks."

"It looks new. You might want to think about wearing something else."

"Why?"

"We'll be playing touch football, so it might get dirty," I explain nervously.

"Football! I can't wait." Her eyes gleam with excitement. "I loved playing football with the neighborhood kids, growing up. I'm probably not as fast as I was then, but I can still throw a spiral."

I laugh, relaxing. "I know what you mean. I might have to have a time-out to catch my breath."

"And no worries about this raggedy old sweater. This is one of my favorites." She rubs her sleeve. "I've sewn a few rips and holes in it already, but I love the way it feels. It's so soft. Here—feel."

I reach with my right hand and gently rub her extended arm.

"Wow. It is." Impulsively, I leave my hand on her arm.

To my surprise, she places her hand over mine. "Do I need to bring anything?"

The warmth from her hand runs up my arm, reminding my body of what I've been missing. "Nothing—only you."

"Okay." She squeezes my hand. "I'm ready!"

So far, so good.

As I turn onto the road out of her driveway and we pass farmland, I ask, "Tell me, how long have you lived in the country?"

"About eight years."

"That's about the same time you started your company, right?"

"Yeah. You remembered."

I glance over at her. She's smiling. "Where did you live before?"

"Actually"—she points straight ahead—"right down the road in a house with more land."

"Did you live alone?" Silence. Oops.

"Um...no. I lived with my partner at the time."

"Oh. Uh, sorry. You want to change the subject?"

"No. It's okay." She takes a deep breath. "We were together for about ten years. As my brother mentioned at dinner, he had a drinking problem. And since I'm his only family, and he had alienated everyone else he ever knew or loved, I was the one he always called when he was in trouble. It could be at all hours of the night, not making any sense because he was blind drunk."

"That must have been hard on your relationship."

"Yeah, he's all I have. I wasn't going to shut him out of my life. Anyway, when I wanted to start my own business, let's just say she wasn't keen on the idea."

Wow. Ten years. Mine only lasted three. "So…she left you?"

Bri is staring out the side window. "There it is." She points to a small, white, two-story house with black shutters at the end of a long driveway. "You know, you meet someone you want to spend a lifetime with and think it will all work out until something comes up, and suddenly that dream of a lifetime is over."

I don't know how to respond. "Does she still live there?"

"No, she moved out about five years ago. Olivia gave me an ultimatum: the business or her."

Well, we have that in common: knowing how it feels to be left by the person who supposedly loves you.

"And you chose the business? And your brother?"

She turns toward me with a smile. "Yes, I did." She turns back to look out the window. "I guess you could say I left her."

"I'm sorry."

"No need to be sorry. We grew apart and didn't want the same things. I think Olivia used the ultimatum as a way of ending the relationship. I never met her expectations. She always wanted a better car, a bigger house, and a bigger bank account. On my salary, that was impossible."

"Did Olivia work?"

"Oh, yeah, as a nurse. Her paycheck went to clothes and expensive wine."

"Ah. Here we are." I say, pulling into my sister's driveway.

But Bri stays in the car and turns to me. "So we sold the house, she got half and the car. I downsized and went into debt to start the business at the age of fifty-six. And now, eight years later, the business is thriving, and I'm doing very well."

"Has there been anyone since Olivia?"

"No. I thought I was in love with her—well, I *was* in love with her—but like I said, we grew apart and had different goals.

I wanted to start couples counseling, but she didn't want to go. I gave her everything I could, and it still wasn't enough."

"So…"

"It all led to the ultimatum. And by that time, I had given up on love, and chose the business."

"Are you glad you made that choice?"

She smiles again, getting out of the car. "Yes. It was the right decision for me."

I wonder what it would take for her to believe in love again. *What would it take for me to believe in love again?*

She opens my door and sticks her head back into the car. "You coming?"

I catch up to her and we walk arm in arm to meet my family.

CHAPTER TWENTY-ONE

Izzy comes flying out the front door. "Aunt Ren! Mom told me you were bringing a girlfriend."

"This is Brianna, who is a girl who is a…friend. Brianna, this is my niece, Isabel."

Izzy stands with her hands on her hips. "You can call me Izzy."

"Well, Izzy, good to meet you." Izzy shakes Bri's extended hand. "You can call me Bri." She turns back to me. "She looks like you. The hair and smile."

"Everyone says we all look alike!" Izzy exclaims. "Me, Mom, and Aunt Ren with our brown hair, eyes, and narrow noses."

"And don't forget the high cheekbones," Bri adds, winking at me.

A young girl sticks her head out from behind Izzy. "Oh, this is my best friend, Ashley. You can call her Ash. This is my Aunt Ren and her girlfriend, Bri. Right?"

"Yes. Right. Nice to meet you, Ash."

"Come on." Izzy waves her hand for us to come in. "We need to pick sides for the football game."

Izzy and Ash zoom into the house, leaving us in their dust.

"What bundles of energy," Bri says.

"Yeah. Uh—sorry about the girlfriend thing."

She smiles like a Cheshire cat.

"I mean, she probably means a girl...who is a friend...not a girlfriend. A girlfriend...like her and Ashley, you know what I mean?"

"What, you don't want me to be your girlfriend?" She laughs, her eyes sparkling.

I smack her shoulder. "Stop it. You're teasing me."

"Hey!" She rubs her arm. "That's my throwing arm. You trying to disable the competition?"

Laughing, I grab her hand and pull her down the hall into the family room, to Clare and Ryan sitting on the couch.

"Bri, I'm glad to meet you. Please join us," Ryan says, standing.

"Your home is lovely. I love the openness, and the French doors are exquisite."

"Ryan designed and built it," Clare explains. "He's the boss, and I do the books."

"You did this house?" Bri asks, her jaw dropping.

Izzy and Ash burst through the back doors. "Come on, time for football!" Izzy yells, waving her arms.

"Can you wait a minute? We're meeting Aunt Ren's girlfriend," Clare says, with raised eyebrows and a smirk on her face as she says the word *girlfriend*.

I give her my evilest eye.

"Come on, people! Let's pick teams and play. You like to play, right, Bri?" Izzy asks.

The teams end up being Bri, Clare, and Ash on the pink team against the yellow team of Ryan, Izzy, and me.

"Everyone warm enough?" Clare asks.

"This is perfect football weather—cold, but not too cold. Brisk. Sun is shining. I'm ready," Ryan says, rubbing his hands together.

The orange cones designate the end zones, and our pink and yellow flags hang out of our back pockets.

"Now, remember, this is *touch* football. Not tackle," Clare reminds us.

"Yes, Mom," Ryan and Izzy respond in unison.

In the first play, Clare carries the football, running toward the end zone with Ryan and Izzy in hot pursuit. Ryan dives for Clare's pink flag but misses and lands with a grunt. Izzy zooms by, grabbing Clare's flag. "Got it!"

Fifteen minutes later, Clare and Bri sprint after Izzy, who zigs and zags with her yellow flag flaring out of her pocket. Clare trips and falls to her knees, breathing heavily. Bri lunges as she makes a last-ditch effort to grab the flag, landing with a groan.

Izzy crosses into the end zone, yelling, "Touchdown!" and spikes the ball.

Ryan and I embrace Izzy. "Way to weave in and out, kiddo!" Ryan says.

"Just like we practiced, right, Dad?"

"Right," he says, high-fiving Izzy.

With the sun setting and the temperature dropping, we play until the score ties after forty-five minutes. I'm sweating and I realize I haven't had this much fun in a long time. I miss the feeling of...I don't know, contentment? I'm usually fighting self-doubt, but right now, I feel like I can conquer the world. It has to be the endorphins from the exercise.

Clare stands with her hands on her hips and says, "Okay, the next score wins. We need to heat up the soup and make the chicken wings."

Without thinking, I pull both of my sleeves up to my elbows. I bend down to hike the ball to Ryan with Izzy to my left. Across from me is Ash, with Clare and Bri on either side.

Suddenly, Ash points to my arm with the scars and says, "What's that on your arm? It's gross."

My mouth drops open. I stare up at Ryan and Clare, who stand like statues, eyes wide. I'm not sure what to say. Finally, I turn to Bri, who surveys my arm before her eyes rise to meet mine.

Studying me, she says to Ash, "Doesn't look ugly to me. It's just different."

But Izzy stands nose-to-nose with Ash. "It is not gross. She got *hurt*." Tears form in her eyes. "It's *not gross*."

"Girls," Clare says, reaching for Izzy.

"She's my aunt, and she's brave. She saved my *life*. How dare you call her arm gross?"

Bri makes the time-out hand gesture. "Izzy, Ash. Enough."

Izzy stands with her arms across her chest, staring at Ash. Ash stares back, her arms crossed.

Bri reaches for my hand. "Will you join us?"

What does she want me to do? I grab her hand and move next to her. She puts her hand on my back.

"Ash, now that you understand that Renata's burned her arm, do you want to ask her any questions?"

My heart starts to race. I feel an anxiety attack looming.

Bri's hand begins to circle my back. She leans toward me, her lips an inch from my ear. "Take a deep breath. You can do this."

I deeply inhale and exhale twice, counting to five as I do.

"Does it hurt?" Ash asks hesitantly.

I take another deep breath. "Sometimes, when I forget to put lotion on it."

"Do you put lotion on your arm every day?" Bri asks.

"Yes."

"Why is it bumpy and stuff?" Izzy asks.

I'm surprised that Izzy asked a question. But then, she's only seen the scars on my hand and neck. I take another deep breath. Bri continues to rub my back. Clare and Ryan both join us.

"Well, these"—I point to my left arm—"are called hypertrophic scars because the skin is raised. It was purple, but now they're paler, even though it still doesn't match my skin."

"Why do you have them?" Ash asks.

"I have them because"—*please don't stop rubbing my back, I need your touch*—"because"—I swallow hard—"I was in a fire."

Ash's eyes widen, and her hands cover her mouth. "Ouch. That must have really hurt."

"I don't know."

"Why not?"

I look to Clare, who nods in encouragement. "Well, I was unconscious."

Bri turns to all of us and asks, "Does anyone else have a scar?" Then she sits on her butt, pulls up her jeans, and pulls down her sock. "Here's one of mine."

I chuckle a little when her blue sock shows Snoopy and the whole gang, including Woodstock, playing football. There are two long scars over her ankle.

"What happened?" Ryan asks.

"Broke my ankle sliding into second base during a softball game." Bri pulls up her sleeve and shows a small rectangular scar on her forearm.

"What's that one?" Izzy asks.

"Skin graft. I cut the tip of my finger in a food processor." She points to the tip of her middle finger on her right hand. "You can see the tip is missing."

"Here's mine," Ryan says, showing us a scar between his thumb and index finger. "I cut it on a table saw."

"Mine," Clare says, pointing to her eyebrow, "is from your Aunt Ren when she threw a softball and hit me in the eye."

I turn to Clare in surprise. "I did not."

"Yes, you did," Clare jabs back.

"I did not."

"Ladies," Ryan says.

Clare pushes my shoulder and says, "Yes, you did."

I smile.

Bri turns to Ash and asks, "Do you have any scars, Ash?"

"Yeah. Look." Ash pulls up her pants and shows everyone a scar on her knee. "I fell off my bike."

"So, you see"—Bri turns and makes eye contact with each of us—"we all have a scar. Right? And they make us stronger because we've survived the things that hurt us."

"Aunt Ren is the best survivor. She has more scars than any of us," Izzy states, putting her hand on my shoulder.

"I agree," Bri says as she gets back onto her knees and continues to massage my back.

Ash hangs her head. "I'm sorry I said it was gross."

I take another deep breath as I reach for Ash's hand. "I accept your apology. And"—I shake my head—"just so you know, when I saw the scars for the first time, I thought they were gross too."

"You did?" Ash raises her head so our eyes meet.

"Yeah. But I'm starting to see them differently." I touch Bri's thigh. "And I hope that if you have any more questions, you'll ask me."

"I will," Ash says.

I grab Izzy, pull her into a hug, and say, "You, too, Izzy."

Izzy smiles. "Okay."

"Right, who's hungry?" Ryan asks.

We all raise our hands and yell at once, "Me!"

"Let's go in and get dinner started," Clare says, grabbing the girls' hands and leading them into the house, Ryan following.

I stay beside Bri, her hand still circling my back, my hand still on her thigh.

"You okay?" she asks.

I gaze into her eyes and rub my other thumb over her cheek. "Thank you." On a whim, I lean in and kiss her cheek. "Ready to eat?"

"I'm starving!"

"Let's go," I say, leaping up.

"I'm not sure I can get up." She points to her ankle. "Too long in one position."

"Here." I extend my arm. "Grab my hand." I pull her up, not letting her hand go as she stands on one foot and twirls her ankle a few times. "Better?"

She studies our hands, fingers entwined. "Much better."

We walk toward the laughter coming from the house.

CHAPTER TWENTY-TWO

"Clare, the soup was delicious. What was the name again?" Bri asks.

"Portuguese chouriço and kale. A recipe passed down from my great-grandmother," Clare answers as she collects the silverware from the table. "You all go into the family room!"

Bri gets up and gathers the bowls as I gather the glasses.

"Please, Bri, go sit down. You're a guest."

"I appreciate your hospitality and the good food—or, I should say, outstanding food. Living alone, it's hard to cook for one person, so this was a treat for me. What is chouriço?"

"Chouriço is the pork sausage in the soup. You blend it with vinegar, salt, paprika, and garlic," I say, stacking the dishwasher.

"Well, it was fabulous."

"I can finish the dishes later," Clare says with a smile. "Let's get to the family room."

Bri sits next to me on the couch. Clare joins Ryan on the love seat. "Where are the girls?" Bri asks.

"In Izzy's bedroom, doing whatever ten-year-olds do," Ryan jokes.

Clare turns to Bri. "So, Ren tells us you own a virtual reality company."

"Yes. I own—well, owned—the company with three other people."

"Ren told us it's about to be acquired, not sold?" Clare asks.

"Yes, it's an acquisition. Another VR company we've worked with over the years will acquire us, but we will keep the same structure and employees. We'll share control of the company."

"Does the company pay you for your stock? How does that work?" Ryan asks.

"They'll pay us for three-quarters of our current stock, and we will substitute the other quarter with the new company shares."

"Sounds lucrative," Clare muses.

"You'll stay with the company?" Ryan asks, grabbing Clare's hand.

"Yes, I'll continue as president until I retire in three years— or sooner. Who knows?"

"What did you do before this?" Clare asks, curious.

"I was a therapist, specializing in structural family therapy."

"Really? Why did you leave the profession?" Clare asks.

"I still renew my license every two years, just in case," Bri admits with a wry smile. "But I wanted a change. Family therapy can be draining."

My gut clenches. I knew Bri was a therapist. But for some reason, I hadn't put the pieces together. Does she see me as someone who needs to be fixed? I clear my throat abruptly. "I hate to be a party pooper, but I have an early meeting in the morning." I turn to her. "You ready to go?"

If she is surprised, she doesn't show it. "Sure."

"Izzy," Clare yells, "Aunt Ren and Bri are leaving."

Izzy and Ash sprint out of the bedroom, holding Nerf guns. Bouncing on her toes, Izzy says, "Bye, Aunt Ren. Thanks for coming. We had fun playing football. Nice to meet you, Bri."

Ash adds, "Yeah, it was fun."

"Good to meet you, Izzy and Ash," Bri says. They both rush back to the bedroom. "Izzy is a fun kid. Energetic too."

"Yeah, no doubt about that. She keeps us on our toes," Ryan says, grinning.

At the door, I hug Ryan and Clare and say, "Thanks, sis, I needed this—the food and company."

"I enjoyed meeting both of you," Bri says, grinning, "and I want a football rematch."

"Anytime. You're always welcome," Ryan says, smiling back.

As we turn to leave, Clare taps Bri on the shoulder, embraces her, and whispers something in her ear. Bri smiles and hugs her back.

As I watch my family interact with her, I say to myself, *Thanks, Darlene, for pushing me because inviting Bri to meet my family seemed the natural thing after spending time with her and her family.* All I know is that this was fun, playing football and having dinner. It warms my heart.

As I back out of the driveway, I ask, "So, what did my sister whisper to you?"

"Oh, nothing."

"Come on. Tell me!"

"I had a fun time today. Thanks for inviting me."

"Don't change the subject."

"The food—can you cook like your sister?"

"Yes," I say firmly. "Now tell me what she said."

It's hard to see her face in the dashboard light, but I think she has a smirk on her face as she asks, "So, I'm assuming you're Portuguese?"

"Yes." I slap her thigh lightly. "Now tell me! What did Clare say?"

I keep my hand on her thigh, surprising even myself.

"You really want to know, huh?"

"Yes, I really do."

I feel Bri's eyes on me. "She said thank you, and that she hasn't seen you smile like this in a long time."

A pause. "Oh."

I drive in silence as my mind goes back to the football game when Bri rubbed my back and my body relaxed and warmed at her touch. In my head, Clare says, *You need to be authentic and communicate.*

I turn to her. My heart pounds. I can do this. I keep my eyes on the road as I say, "Thank you for rubbing my back and keeping me in the moment earlier."

Bri places her hand on top of mine. "Well, first, I took a chance by asking you to join me in front of the girls. You did. You were brave." She squeezes my hand. "You had no idea what I was going to do."

"Yeah." I glance at her. "You can say that again. My heart felt like it was going to jump out of my chest."

"I could tell by your breathing. It was the same way you were breathing that day at school, in the hallway."

"Yeah. Anxiety attack."

"I gathered as much from Izzy's comments, and I drew some conclusions about your scars. I followed my instincts. Over the years, they've not misled me." Bri chuckles. "Well, maybe except for Olivia—my ex."

"Well, you live and you learn, right?"

"Yeah, I guess so." Bri pauses and says, "So, back to you. I rubbed your back to signal I was there to support you."

"Thank you. I felt your support." I squeeze her thigh. "I appreciated it."

Bri looks down, removes her hand from mine, takes a deep breath, and says, "Okay. Let me ask you: Any higher aspirations? Like superintendent? Turn left here," she says as we approach a stop sign.

"No way." I shake my head. "No way." I pull into her driveway and put the car in park.

"You want to come in?"

"Um—" Why am I hesitating? I need to slow down. She's a therapist. I'm her project. "Um…no, but can I walk you to your door?"

"Sure, I'd like that," Bri says lightly.

As we walk to the door, I look around. "It sure is dark and quiet out here in the country."

We hear howls, followed by high-pitched barks and yips. Eyes wide, I jerk my head toward the sound. "What is that?"

She laughs. "Coyotes."

"Are they close?"

Bri points toward the back of the house. "Behind the house in the woods." She touches my arm. "You're safe. When there's a full moon, it's almost as bright as day."

I want to spend time with her. Why am I hesitating? She is not Maggie.

"I'd like to see it with you."

"See the coyotes?"

"No!" I laugh. "The full moon."

"Okay. I'll check the calendar, and you can come for dinner and stare at the moon with me." As we reach the door, Bri turns and gently runs her hands up and down my arms. "I had a wonderful time with you today."

My breath hitches. "So did I." I focus on her lips.

A coyote howls in the distance. Then silence.

"May I kiss you?" she asks finally.

Her face is close to mine. My adrenaline skyrockets. "Y-yes. I'd like that."

Her left hand moves to my neck as she presses her lips to mine, soft and tender. Her kiss is gentle at first, then adds pressure, sending heat down my spine. Her tongue swipes across my top lip before she pulls away.

Panting slightly, she says, "I felt that down to my toes."

My head is spinning. "I enjoyed it too," I say, taking a step back. "Can we, um, do this again?"

Her eyes widen. "Kiss? Sure." She leans in for another.

I push her back with a slight touch of my hand on her chest. "No. Yes. I mean—when can I see you again?"

Bri covers her mouth. "Oops. Sorry."

I touch her arm. "I definitely want another kiss. But...you need to...I need to go slow."

She steps back. With sincerity in her eyes, she says, "Ren, I am in no hurry. I want to spend time with you to get to know you better, and if kissing happens to be involved occasionally, I won't complain."

"Okay." I kiss her nose. "I gotta go. Call me tomorrow?"

"Sure."

I turn back to her. "And thank you for the back rub and for making me smile."

CHAPTER TWENTY-THREE

"Late night?" Darlene asks as we walk into the school building, students congregating on the steps in the commons.

"Morning, Ms. Santos."

"Morning, Seth."

"Morning, Ms. Santos and Ms. Meyers."

"Morning, Cindy. Did you submit that college application?" Darlene asks.

"Yup! Keep your fingers crossed," Cindy responds as she passes us.

Darlene crosses her fingers and raises them in the air so Cindy can see them. "She will be successful, no matter what she pursues," she muses to me.

A student bumps into me with their backpack, turns, and says, "Sorry, Ms. Santos."

"Hey, Kevin, no worries. I'm glad you bumped into me—I saw your pencil drawing of the elephant and her calf in the art wing. It's amazing."

"Thanks!"

"Are you entering it in the regional art exhibition competition?"

"Uh, I don't know. Ms. Boyer is encouraging me to."

"Well, you have my vote."

"Thanks." He smiles sheepishly.

I wave him on.

My phone rings. It might be Bri. It keeps ringing.

"Are you gonna answer your phone?"

"Good morning. This is Ms. Santos."

"Good morning, Ms. Santos," Bri says, her voice low and sexy on the other end.

A thrill shoots up my spine. "Bri. It's you."

"It's me."

The students pick up their pace as the bell rings. I turn my body so a student misses running me over. "Can you hold a sec?"

"Sure."

Finally, the bell stops.

"Okay, now I can hear you."

"I wanted to tell you again how much I enjoyed spending time with you and your family," Bri says.

"Me too." I walk into my office. Darlene stops at the entrance and stretches her neck into my office, mouthing, *Is it Brianna?* When I nod, she gives me a thumbs-up as she moves on.

"So...I checked the calendar, and there'll be a full moon in two weeks."

I smile. "You checked already?"

"Already? I couldn't wait. In two weeks—Saturday. Can you join me?"

"Probably."

"I'll cook dinner for you—uh, for us. While my cooking is not as wonderful as your sister's, I *can* follow a recipe. Do you have a favorite meal?"

I blush. "Gosh. Um...surprise me."

"Ugh." She laughs. "I was hoping you wouldn't say that. Do you have any allergies or any food you can't eat?"

"None. I'll eat anything except coconut."

"No coconut. Got it."

"Can I bring anything?"

"Nope. Just your appetite and some warm clothes to sit and gaze at the moon."

"I will. I'm looking forward to it."

"Me too. Okay, I gotta go. We're meeting with the acquisition company this morning. I'd best be off."

I raise a hand to my lips, remembering last night's kiss. I'm not sure I can wait. Why don't I call Bri back and invite her to my place for pizza and a movie?

"Renata. Earth to Renata," Darlene says.

I snap out of it. "Sorry, what?"

"We need to leave in about ten minutes to get to the board office for the budget meeting."

"Right."

Darlene sits in the chair next to my desk. "Did something happen this weekend?"

"Why do you ask?"

"There's a sparkle in your eyes. What happened?" Darlene teases.

I roll my eyes. "Give me a break. It was the usual Sunday. I went to dinner with Clare and her family. And we played touch football."

"Anything else? Did you invite a certain Ms. Walsh?" Her eyes study me with piercing scrutiny.

I swivel in my chair, avoiding eye contact with her and hold back a smile.

"You did! I can tell. You did."

"Okay." I swivel back to face Darlene. "Yes. Bri went with me, and we had a great time."

"And after dinner…?"

"Really? Do you have no shame?"

"Nope, I want the details," Darlene says, rubbing her hands together.

I laugh. "There are none. We had a good time, I took her home, we kissed, I left."

Her eyes light up. "Oh yeah? And how was the kiss?"

"Not here."

"Come on. Give me a hint."

I put my face in my hands. "I was actually daydreaming about it when you walked in." I feel the heat warm my face.

"That satisfying, huh?"

"Yes. And maybe you should take the next step with Shelly so you can experience a satisfying kiss firsthand instead of dragging the details out of me," I tease her, straightening in my chair. "Now let's hustle to that budget meeting."

* * *

On our way back from the meeting, Darlene says, "Sarah Reynolds and I are getting together this weekend."

I'm surprised. "Really? Is that a good thing, since we're doing business with them?"

"As *friends*, Ren." She gives me a look and shrugs. "I know it's kind of not the norm, but we hit it off. We both come from a military family and moved around a lot. We're both the youngest with two older brothers. And one of her brothers is gay too. We have a lot in common."

I think about it. "I guess it's not like we have the final decision whether the school moves forward with VR anyway."

"Right. Sarah says she needs a break from her two children and husband, so we're going for a drink and dinner. You want to join us?"

I tilt my head. "No, thanks. You and Sarah have a good time." I smile because I'm hoping to have other plans. "I think I'm going to ask Bri over to my place."

"You go, girl!"

CHAPTER TWENTY-FOUR

Later in the week, as I sit watching the television, absentmindedly scrolling through my phone, I feel an overwhelming urge to call Bri. Should I invite her over on Saturday night? What if she sees me as someone who needs to be helped because of the scars? But what if she doesn't? The way Bri looks at me and how I feel when we're together—there's something there that can't be denied. But am I brave enough to find out what it is?

It rings two times, three times. Maybe she's not home from work. Four times.

"Hello?"

"Hi, Bri? This is Ren. You busy?"

She laughs. "No, I was moving a fifty-pound salt block to my water softener."

"Fifty pounds?"

"Yes."

I imagine Bri in a tank top and shorts, squatting and lifting, her muscles flexing and straining as she lifts the salt blocks. My face gets hot.

"You still there?" she asks.

"Sorry, yeah. You lift fifty-pound salt blocks?"

"Someone has to do it." She clears her throat. "Um, thanks for not hanging up. You've been on my mind all day."

I smile to myself. "To be honest, I've been thinking about you too."

Silence.

"Uh, I want to ask you something."

"Sure."

I glide my hand over my neck, arm, and the top of my hand, aware of the thick, raised skin through my long-sleeved T-shirt.

"Are you there?" she asks.

"I was wondering if you'd like to come to my house Saturday night for pizza and a movie." I hold my breath, waiting.

"Yes! Sorry, I sound too eager, and you want to go slow. Ask me again."

I laugh. "Would you like to join me Saturday night for pizza and a movie?"

"Um…what movie?"

"I don't know."

"What kind of pizza?"

"Either Marion's or Donato's."

"I'll need to check my schedule. Can you hold?"

"Okay, okay." I laugh. "Do you want to come or not?"

Her voice suddenly low and smoky, Bri says, "An interesting question."

My mind creates a picture of her underneath me, her legs wrapped around my waist, screaming my name as she arches into me. I do believe she's flirting with me.

Flustered, I say, "Uh…see you at six. Bring whatever you want to drink."

"Will do. Again, thanks for calling. Good night, Renata. Sweet dreams."

"Good night, Bri."

I look at my phone after we hang up. She is flirting with me, right? I hope so.

CHAPTER TWENTY-FIVE

While I open the pizza boxes, Bri asks, "What movie are we watching?" as she dumps the ice in the ice bucket.

"*The Heat* with Sandra Bullock and Melissa McCarthy," I reply. "Darlene told me it's hilarious. Have you seen it?" I ask, glancing at Bri, leaning against the kitchen counter.

"No, but I've wanted to because Sandra Bullock is one of the leading ladies. She was hot in *Miss Congeniality*."

"Oh, a Sandra Bullock admirer," I say, smiling. "Food update. Everything is here on the counter—pizza, paper plates, chips, pretzels, dip, and, of course"—I open the bag—"peanut M&M's. I'm addicted to them."

Bri sits on the couch, her plate on her lap as I find Prime Video.

I point to the space next to Bri on the sofa and ask, "May I?"

"Please."

I keep a little distance between us. She stretches and crosses her legs at her ankles, which is when I spot her red, purple, orange, and green socks.

I turn to her. "What is it with you and socks?"

She turns her foot from side to side. "They show my fun, adventurous side."

"Well, I can't wait to see more."

She wiggles her eyebrows. "See more of what? My leg or my socks?"

I slap her arm. "Stop!"

I locate the movie I rented earlier and hit play.

We laugh throughout the movie until we pause to collect empty plates. I curl my legs underneath me and lean against Bri, who puts her arm over the couch behind me and asks, "Ready for act two?"

"Yeah, I haven't laughed this hard in months. Thanks for joining me."

As we continue watching the movie, Bri leans in, her breath tickling my ear as she says, "They have such good chemistry."

I don't turn. I'm afraid of what I'll see in her eyes. I feel her body heat engulfing me from our bodies touching. I swallow hard and whisper, "They do."

She drops her hand so it's resting on my shoulder. I turn slowly, and her blue eyes meet mine, penetrating my soul.

She squeezes my shoulder and turns back to the movie. Under her touch, the tension in my muscles disappears, and my eyes slowly close.

A loud noise wakes me up. "What was that?" I ask, groggy.

"The car exploded."

I turn to the TV. A car is on fire, flames reaching the sky.

Fire. My heart begins to palpitate. My breathing is ragged. I jump up from the couch, sweat droplets forming on my forehead.

"I—need—to—" I race through the dining room and jerk open the front door. The cold hits me like I just walked into a freezer. In my front yard, I take deep breaths, hands behind my head as I walk in circles. The corner streetlight is the only illumination.

As I circle, I tell myself, *Calm down. You are okay. The car fire was a trigger. Calm down.* A creaking sound attracts my attention. I turn.

Bri stands outside on the front porch. "Ren. What can I do?" Her voice is so soothing. The headlights of a car cross over her face, showing concern.

Between uneven breaths, I say, "Nothing. Go back into the house." I keep walking in a circle.

"Ren. What do you need?"

I need you to hold me.

"Please, Bri. I don't want you to see me this way."

"What way?" she asks with puzzlement on her face.

"Anxiety attack. Weak. Out of control."

She shakes her head. "I don't understand. You perceive yourself as weak?"

"Well, what would you call it?" My voice goes up a notch. "Ms. Therapist!"

She moves toward me slowly, one step at a time. "I'm going to ignore that last statement."

"Well, isn't it true? You're trying to analyze me?" I tell myself to stop.

When she touches my arm, I pull away.

"Okay," she says slowly. "Now you don't want me to touch you?"

"Go back inside!"

She takes a step back. In the dim light, I recognize the hurt in her eyes.

"Ren. I'm here because I care about you. A lot." She takes another step back. "But it appears you're not ready for someone to care about you." She turns back into the house, the creaky door closing behind her.

CHAPTER TWENTY-SIX

I gaze up to the dark, cloudless sky. What do I need? Why does she care about me? Jesus Christ, Renata, pull yourself together.

I go back into the house and walk into the kitchen. Bri is in the living room, putting on her coat.

"Bri, wait—please. I guess the noise from the explosion on the TV woke me up. I saw the fire. I was confused as to where I was, and it caused an anxiety attack."

"I understand, Renata. First, I can't image what you went through. And second, I'm starting to really care about you. Let me be there for you." She raises her hands. "You know what? Never mind. I forgot that you only see me as a therapist. I think I'll be going. You enjoy the rest of the movie. Thanks for the pizza."

I push the door open, and in three long strides, I'm at the driveway just as Bri opens her car door. "Bri. Wait. Please."

She stops and stands, looking over the roof of her car, her elbow on the car door. "Yes, Renata?" Her face is expressionless.

Clare's voice reverberates in my head. *Communication and authenticity.* I raise my chin and look straight into her eyes. "I—I need you to stay."

We stare at each other, neither of us breaking eye contact.

"Fine. I'll stay." She closes her door and walks with me back into the house.

For the remainder of the movie, Bri and I sit apart and don't say a word to each other. I move closer but never close enough to reach out and touch her.

When the movie finally finishes, Bri grabs her coat and says, "I best be going."

I'm close enough to her to touch her. "Let me help you with your coat."

"No, I got it. Thanks." Bri turns toward the door.

I touch her shoulder. She turns to me, so I ask hopefully, "Are we still on next week for dinner and watching the full moon?"

"I don't know. I hope we are. But it's up to you."

"Goddammit, Bri." I push my hair back in frustration. "I'm trying here. Do you understand how hard it is for me to open up, to let someone see me?" I point to my chest. "To let them in?"

Bri looks me squarely in the eyes. "No. I don't. How can I when you won't talk to me?"

"I'm not ready to talk about it."

Our eyes remain locked as silence takes over the room.

I watch as Bri's face relaxes, her eyes changing from frustration to understanding.

Finally, she takes my hand. "Well, telling me you're not ready to talk is a start."

"That's enough?"

"Is it the truth? You're not ready?"

"Yes." I squeeze her hand.

"All I need from you is to be honest with me." She rubs her thumb over my hand, and I realize she's holding the hand with the scars. I don't pull away.

Bri holds my chin and tilts it upward. Anticipating her lips on mine makes my head spin.

My hands go behind her neck when our lips meet, and I feel her tremble.

CHAPTER TWENTY-SEVEN

Saturday morning, I busy myself with laundry and trying to calm my thoughts about last weekend's movie night. I fold a long-sleeved shirt and drop it into the clothes basket before carrying it to my bedroom, peering out the window as I pass through the dining room. It's snowing.

My phone alerts me to a text.

Morning, Ren.

Good morning, Bri.

We might not be able to see the full moon with the snow. Do you still want to come over?

I don't have to.

Don't be silly 😊 *I want you to come over. I'm cooking dinner too, remember?*

I hesitate, my fingers unmoving. Finally, I type, *Yes. I still want to have dinner with you.*

Dinner will be ready between 6 and 6:30. Hopefully.

Hopefully?

You never can tell with me cooking. Come over any time.

Will do.

Bye xx

After spending most of the day catching up on schoolwork, I peek out the picture window in the dining room. Giant snowflakes are still falling. There are over three inches on the ground. The roads and yards are white, and only tire tracks line the streets.

I glance at my watch. Four thirty p.m. I want to spend time with Bri, but driving might not be a good idea if I wait much longer. She *did* say I can come over any time.

I quickly dress. I inspect myself in the full-length mirror: gray pants, a white, long-sleeved blouse, and my collar peeking out from under my gray sweater. Do I look sexy?

I run my hands down the sides of my body. Yes, I do. I make sure my collar and hair hide the scars on my left ear and neck and gather my winter coat, scarf, and gloves from the hall closet, the bottle of wine from the kitchen counter.

I have no problem driving through the snowy roads, especially since I'm going ten miles below the speed limit. I turn slowly onto the road leading to Bri's house.

A classic winter scene appears—tree branches hanging low from the heavy snow. Her porch light sends rays through the falling snowflakes, making them sparkle like diamonds.

I park in her driveway and knock on the door. No response. I knock again. No response.

I glance through the window. There is a vaulted ceiling with wooden beams, earth-tone walls, and hickory kitchen cabinets. Bri is standing over a counter, and muffled music escapes through the window.

I knock again. No answer. My feet are getting cold. Calling out, I enter a foyer with a mirror on one wall and an antique coatrack with a seat against the other.

Sara Bareilles's "I Choose You" blasts down the foyer. Bri is singing but not quite hitting the right notes, which makes me both cringe and smile. I stop in the middle of the great room and admire her.

Her back is to me, bending over as she wipes the far counter. She's wearing black sweatpants with gray stripes down the side and a white T-shirt. Her hips sway as she sings, and her broad shoulders bounce up and down to the music.

She turns and points her finger out into the open space in my direction as she sings, "And I choose you."

Her eyes meet mine. She stops singing, and her mouth drops open. Her eyes widen to the size of quarters. "Uh…you're here." She drops her finger.

I grin at her. "Yeah. You told me I could come at any time."

She rubs her hands down her pants. "I did say that, didn't I."

I step into the kitchen, a few feet from her. Flour smudges her cheek, nose, and in the V of her T-shirt, and she has something green in her hair.

I scan the kitchen and smile. There are pans, knives, and cutting boards everywhere—on the counter, piled in the sink. A pot is on the stove, a Crock-Pot on the counter.

"Um." Bri surveys the kitchen. "I didn't expect you this early."

"You move your hips rather well."

"Well…uh…living alone, I sing and dance around the house because, as you could hear, I'm kinda flat. At least, that's what the music teacher told me in high school when I tried out for the choir."

"Well, what about your dancing?"

"Same thing. I tried out for the high school play as an extra in *Oklahoma!* And guess what?"

I smile. "What?"

"The director told me I had two left feet and would I like to be on the stage crew."

"And I bet you were good at it."

"I enjoyed it. Probably more than dancing." Bri spins in a circle, then says, "Let me turn down the music." She rubs her hand on her chin, turning in a circle. "Where is it?"

"Where's what?"

"My phone." She rummages through the pots and pans. "I know it's here somewhere," she mutters as she picks up a pot lid covering. "Found it." As she lowers the volume, she says, "I just started to clean up."

I approach her and reach toward her head.

She takes a step back. "What are you doing?"

I point to her head. "You have something in your hair." I pull it out. "What is it?"

She takes it from me, examining the white and green strip. "Leek."

"How did leek get into your hair?"

"Don't ask." She plops it into her mouth.

I scrunch my face. "You really just ate that?"

"I like leeks."

I raise her chin with my finger. "Flour on your cheek."

"Where?"

"Let me." I rub my hand over her cheek and brush off the flour. My eyes move to her exposed cleavage. "Here's more." I run my hand over the top of her chest from one end of her clavicle to the other.

Bri leans her forehead on mine and touches my hip. "That feels good. But I need to shower, and I can't do that"—she squeezes my hip—"until I finish cleaning up." She turns and finishes wiping down the counter.

"No problem. Can I do anything to help?"

The red blush continues up her neck. I never thought I would hold such power over a woman again.

She swallows hard. "Um…help?"

"Oh." I laugh. "I mean help with"—I point to counter and sink—"all of this. Not the shower."

Bri giggles.

"Anything I can do while you're getting ready?"

"I have white wine in the fridge. And a red or two in the wine rack—I didn't know which you liked. I have bourbon too. Oh," she says as she sees the bottle in my hand, "I see you brought some wine."

"Yeah. A red, just in case."

"Thank you. Uh—by the way." Her eyes move up and down. "You look very sexy."

I look sexy.

"Thank you. You're adorable."

"Stop," Bri says as she spins around. "To help, you can turn the oven on to two fifty and put the bread"—she points to a baguette on the counter—"in to warm. That would be helpful."

"Will do."

She walks out of the kitchen through the great room and turns right.

I take a few steps to follow her. "Bri, if you need any help in the shower, yell."

She stops in her tracks and turns. "Are you teasing me?"

"For now." I wink.

Her head reappears around the corner. "Oh, by the way, I have a treat for you on the side table by the couch." And she disappears.

I walk back to the kitchen and glance in the dining room. The table has two place settings with a candle between the plates. I grab the cookie sheet with the bread on it and put it in the oven. Then I watch the fresh snow continue to build. No moonlight to be seen.

It is so peaceful, the only sound the ticking of a grandmother's clock on a tall hutch in the living room. My mind and body relax.

I wander through the living area and notice a telescope on a tripod standing in front of the French doors leading to the deck. She really is serious about seeing the moon. I turn toward the sofa and my smile widens as I notice a bowl of peanut M&M's on a side table. She remembered. I sigh, my heart warming. She did this all for me.

I grab a handful and plop them into my mouth one at a time as I continue my tour of Bri's house. Just enjoy the moment, I remind myself.

I end up in the front of the house. Off to the right are three shelves full of books, the titles ranging from J. D. Robb to books on virtual reality, autobiographies of famous women, and stargazing.

There is a shuffling behind me. I turn to see Bri heading my way. Her hair is still damp, and she's wearing blue jeans with a white cotton button-down with vertical red strips, the front tucked in with the sleeves rolled up to her elbows. The top buttons show a hint of cleavage.

I catch my breath at the sight of her.

She stops behind me. "I like variety in my reading."

I can feel the radiating warmth of her body. "Yes, I can see that," I mutter, paging through a book to keep my hands occupied so I don't grab her and kiss her.

Bri breaks the silence and says, "Hey, I was thinking while I was showering—Do you want to bring your car into the garage? Then, when you go home, we won't need to brush off all the snow."

"Good idea. I'd appreciate it."

"Okay. Let's move it before we eat."

We do so and reenter the house through the mudroom. I rub my hands together. Bri reaches for them. "They're cold." She rubs her hands around mine. "What was that noise?"

"I think it was my stomach."

Bri smiles, still holding my hands. "I guess you're ready to eat?"

"The smell is making my stomach rumble. What are we having?"

Bri drops her hand, takes my elbow, and guides me to the table, where she pulls out my chair.

"Thank you."

"Nothing special. It's called wintry savory vegetable soup. I'll be right back." After she sets down the bowls, she says, "Bon appétit," and returns to her chair across from me.

"Wow, this is delicious. It's so rich and creamy. What's in it?"

"There's carrots, leeks…" She chuckles. "But you knew that. Onion, potatoes, mushrooms, and lots of cream. Oh, and celery."

I take another spoonful. "It's wonderful."

Bri lifts her spoon to her mouth and stops halfway before she drops her spoon. "Damn it." She pushes back her chair and gets up. "I forgot the bread!" When she jogs to the kitchen, I hear her yell, "Ouch. Damn it!" She returns with the baguette, sucking on three fingers.

"Are you okay?"

"Yeeessss," she mumbles.

"Baguettes are my favorite."

"Good. Then my burned fingers are worth it." Suddenly, she stares at me, looking like a deer in headlights. "I'm so sorry. I—burned—" She holds up her three fingers. "My—your—I didn't mean to—"

"Stop." I reach across the table and touch her burnt fingers. "Bri. I'm fine." I don't feel my stomach tightening or my breath changing "Let's eat."

CHAPTER TWENTY-EIGHT

During dinner we talk about our high school and college experiences.

"Well," I begin, "I played volleyball in high school and college, along with being in student government in high school."

"Me too. My senior year, I was president."

"So was I." Something else we have in common: sports and being leaders. "How about college?" I ask.

"I never thought about going to college because no one in my family ever did. My grades weren't bad, probably a C average."

"So how did you wind up going to college?"

"I worked as a lifeguard after my junior year, and the director of the pool was also the athletic director of a small college, Eastern. Unbeknownst to me, she followed my senior year and then asked me to come to Eastern."

I take a sip of my soup. "I assume you went, right?"

"Yeah, I got a scholarship—well, not really a scholarship, because back in the midseventies, I got grants and worked as the women's athletic director's secretary."

"So you played…?"

"Field hockey." Bri butters a piece of baguette. "And basketball and softball, just like in high school. When I was a sophomore, I realized I was smart and enjoyed learning. How about you?"

"I can't image playing three sports in college. How did you do it?" I ask Bri.

"Well, even in high school, I played three sports. That was the norm back then."

"I went to Eastern Kentucky on a volleyball scholarship—I was a setter—and got my degree in education and then my master's at the University of Dayton. And went into debt." I laugh.

"I got my master's in counseling at Wright State and also went into debt, but probably not as much as you did."

I place my soup spoon down. "Tell me more about your family."

"My dad worked in a factory and my mom as a waitress. They both worked hard and wanted us to have more than they did, so they saved their hard-earned money that added to our grants to send us both to college. And yours?"

"My father was in construction and my mom was an accountant."

Bri laughs then says, "Just like your sister and Ryan."

"Yeah, funny how things work. So how're David and Liz? I really enjoyed meeting them when we had dinner."

Bri sighs.

"Is something wrong?"

Bri stands and rubs the back of her neck as she walks to the front window. "Um…Liz says he's under a lot of stress at work."

I follow and stand next to her, gazing out the window.

"And I always worry he's going to relapse."

"Oh."

"When he attends his AA meetings and talks to his sponsor, he handles his stress appropriately, he's optimistic, he spends time with Liz and friends…"

"And?" I say, grabbing her hand and intertwining our fingers.

"And—I'm sure you know the story. David starts feeling good and thinks he no longer needs that support system, so he doesn't go consistently." Bri shakes her head. "I feel so helpless."

"What do you mean?"

"I talk with him and he tells me he's working the program. But, Liz told me his sponsor, who he's had for five years, moved recently and he hasn't been to a meeting in a while." She sighs. "I'm sure you've experienced addiction issues with some of the students or their families."

"Yeah, but I don't live with the person every day. The helplessness and worry, I imagine, can take a toll on his relationship with his wife and you."

"As far as I'm concerned, Liz is a saint. She stands by him, no matter what. And the last time we talked, they said things were fine, but...It's—I'm—Not sure. Anyway, what about you?"

I squeeze her hand. "If you need someone to talk to about your brother, a sounding board or anything...I'm a good listener."

Her eyes meet mine. "Thanks, I'll keep that in mind." Bri moves into the kitchen, grabs her phone, and asks, "What kind of music do you like?"

"Rock and Broadway musicals."

"Oh? Show tunes. Have you ever been to New York City?"

"No, it's on my bucket list."

"Anything you'd like to see?"

"*Hamilton*," I say with a grin as I follow her into the kitchen.

"Yeah, you and everyone else."

"I know, I know. So what about you? What music do you like, besides Sara Bareilles?"

"I guess my taste is eclectic when it comes to music. I like a little bit of everything. What would you like to listen to while we have dessert?"

"Dessert?"

"Yes." Bri opens the freezer drawer and pulls out two containers of ice cream, one in each hand. "Nothing outlandish. I have chocolate and vanilla. I'm not very exciting when it comes to ice cream."

"You know what you like. I'll have chocolate—and I trust your selection of music."

Bri places the chocolate on the counter, picks an Andrea Bocelli album, and dishes out the ice cream.

CHAPTER TWENTY-NINE

"A perfect meal for this cold weather," I say as I sit on the brown leather sectional.

Bri joins me in the middle section, propping her legs up on the ottoman, covered with business and golf magazines.

I pick up a golf magazine. "Do you golf?"

"I'm not the best, but I hold my own. How about you?"

"I did, but I haven't since my injury."

"Oh. Sorry."

"No need to apologize." I put the magazine back on the ottoman.

"Do you think you'll golf again?" Bri asks.

"Not sure. But I like to hike, and if you do too, maybe we can do that. Not right now—maybe in the spring?"

Her eyes twinkle. "What's wrong with a walk in the winter?"

"Nothing, I guess." I assumed we would be together in the spring. I need to slow down.

"Okay, so when do you want to go?" Bri asks as she reaches for the bowl of M&M's and hands it to me.

"Oh, don't worry, I found them," I laugh. "Thanks for remembering."

"Well." Bri grabs an M&M and holds it up to my mouth and feeds it to me, her fingers softly gazing my lips. Her eyes widen, and my heart skips a beat. Bri's face reddens as she shoves the bowl into my lap. "Have some more."

"You don't have to twist my arm. Back to our winter walk—where would we go?"

"There's a bicycle path. You cross over it about three hundred feet before you hit my driveway."

"Yeah, I remember. I saw the little stop sign for the bikers." I throw the M&M's into my mouth.

"Are you game for a winter walk? Maybe in a few weeks or so?" Bri asks with hopeful eyes.

"I'd like that," I say, joy filling me. "By the way, what time is it?"

Bri looks to the grandmother clock. "About nine thirty. Why? You need to go?"

I look toward the window. "The snow has been falling nonstop for hours. I don't want to get stuck driving home."

"We'd better check." Bri gets up and walks to the front window. I join her, only a few inches behind, inhaling her floral-scented shampoo. "Wow. I'm not sure you're going home tonight."

She turns, her hands falling to my hips. Mine rest on her forearms. We gaze into each other's eyes. All I hear is my heartbeat.

Hesitantly, Bri asks, "Do you...want to stay here tonight? I mean, there must be eight inches out there. The city won't plow until it stops snowing, and they do the main roads first."

What does she mean, stay here? Does she want sex? Am I ready?

Bri returns to the couch, and I move next to her, our thighs touching, and say, "I need to tell you something." I take a deep breath. "I haven't been with anyone since my injury. I'm not sure I'm ready—"

Bri's eyes open wide. "No, no—" She moves so our thighs no longer touch, and right away I miss its warmth. "What are you talking about?"

I'm confused. "You said to stay the night."

"Yeah, meaning driving home in this snow would be dangerous. You can stay. I have a guest bedroom."

"So, you didn't mean…stay to have sex?"

"No."

"So you don't want to have sex with me?" I ask unthinkingly.

"Yes. No. Argh—you make me act so—I'm flustered because I do want to touch you, hold you, and if it leads to making love, then it does or it doesn't."

I grab her hand. She said making love, not sex.

"Let me finish," Bri continues. "Look at me." Bri lifts my head with her hand. I watch her lips as she says, "I like you, Ren. I like spending time with you. I'm thoroughly enjoying tonight." She rubs her thumb over my cheek. "I will wait."

I raise my eyes to meet hers.

Bri straightens, pushes her shoulders back, and drops her hands onto mine. "Seriously, Ren. I can wait until you first of all like me—and like me enough to want me. And, if we need to, we can figure ways to get…your body"—her neck turns blotchy—"reacquainted with touch." She adds without taking a breath, "If that's an issue, I mean. I don't know if it is. I could be way off—"

My body aches for her. "Bri. Stop rambling."

"Oh. Okay." She leans back into the couch, then sits up again. "I'm sorry if I said something to upset you. I didn't want to."

"Bri. Stop."

She leans back again. "Okay."

I hesitate. "Can we start by making out a little?"

Bri perks up. "Sure."

"You are adorable. Do you know that?"

"If you say so. I have only one request," Bri says laughingly. "I need you to tell me if I'm touching you where you don't want to be touched. You can be in control. You can be the director of our make-out scene." As Bri watches me, her eyes flare with desire.

"Go ahead. Run your hand through my hair."

She spreads her long fingers through my hair, slightly pulling at the back.

God, my body feels like it's on fire. I turn my head, exposing my neck, and tell her, "Kiss my neck."

She runs her hand through my hair as she kisses the right side of my neck and adds a quick bite.

"Did I tell you to bite my neck?"

Bri stops. "No, sor—"

"Do it again."

She does, and I feel her panting on my neck.

"Lips. Kiss my lips."

Bri tilts and locks her warm, alluring lips with mine.

"Another," I instruct her when our lips are barely apart.

She extends her tongue between my lips, asking for entrance. I oblige. Our tongues do a tango. Her hand moves toward my scarred left breast.

I grab it and break our kiss. "Did I say you could touch my breast?"

"No." Her head falls.

"Who is the director?"

"You," Bri says, then tilts her head to the side playfully. "Have you been hiding that you're a dominatrix?"

I laugh. "Um...no. But I'm starting to like this." I grab her hand and place it on my right breast. "This one."

I crash into her lips. She starts caressing my breast. My nipple hardens.

"Oh, god. It's been so long," I say between our tongues exploring each other's mouths.

A phone rings.

We continue to kiss, taking turns sucking and biting each other's lower lips. Bri throws her leg onto my lap.

Another ring.

"Should we answer it?" Bri pants as our lips part.

"Whose is it?"

"Yours."

"Damn. I should get it."

Bri removes her leg, and her hand leaves my breast as she collapses back into the couch.

I find my phone on the ottoman and answer, "Hello?"

"Ren, why did it take you so long to answer the phone? Are you okay?" Clare asks as I blush.

"Yes, I'm at Bri's. She made me dinner."

"Oh. I see. Dinner with Bri."

"Claaare."

"Our electricity went out and I was calling to see if yours did. But it seems you can't answer that question since you're not home so I'll just hang up now. Enjoy your evening."

I hit *end* and notice I have twelve voice messages.

I hesitate and listen to the first one.

The male voice. "Where are you?"

I jump off the couch, my voice rising, and yell at the phone, "Who are you?" Then throw it on the couch, almost hitting Bri.

"Ren. Who was that?"

I start to pace.

"I...don't know." My breathing becomes ragged. My heart is racing and not from our recent make-out session.

"Okay," Bri says as she rubs my arm. "Let's stop the anxiety attack. Deep breaths."

"I don't need this. I don't know who it is."

"Deep breaths in, deep breaths out." Bri engulfs me in a warm, gentle hug. I surrender to the safety of her arms, and she moves her hand up and down my back. "Okay. How about we sit down? You want some water?"

I sit back down onto the couch and nod. My breathing returns to normal as Bri hands me a glass.

"Better?"

"Yes. Thank you."

Bri grabs my phone, and I give her my access code. She listens to a few of the voice mails and ends the message. She turns to me, drapes her arm over my shoulder, and with concern on her face, asks, "How long have you been getting these calls?"

"For a couple of months now."

"The one message says he's seen you with a woman and that she can't take care of you as he can."

"Now he knows about you."

"Do you listen to the messages?"

"Not all of them, Some but not the full message."

"You haven't erased them."

"No. I thought if he didn't stop...I don't know..."

"Have you called the police?"

"Not yet."

Bri takes my hands. "Renata, let's call them now."

I shake my head. "What can they do?"

"Do you have any idea who it could be?"

"No."

She squeezes my hand. "Ren, the calls have terrified you. I think it's time to call the police."

"What if it's nothing?"

She wraps my face in her hands, looks directly into my eyes, and says, "You've had how many calls now? Ten to twenty? What about the roses? Could they have been from him?"

My eyes widen. "That did cross my mind when you said you didn't send them. What if they are from him? That means he knows where I work."

"Let's call the police."

I acquiesce.

CHAPTER THIRTY

After contacting the police, Bri leads me to the guest bedroom.

"This is the bedroom. The bath is across the hall, here to your right. My office is the next room, and my bedroom is at the end of the hall."

"Your home is lovely."

"Thanks. I like it. I'll put some towels in the bathroom. Toothbrush and toothpaste are in the medicine cabinet."

I point to my outfit. "Do you have something I could wear to bed?"

Bri's eyes roam from my head to my toes. "Oh yeah. Tank top and shorts? Or do you want sweatpants?"

"Tank top and shorts will work fine."

The bedroom's ice-blue walls have a dreamy quality. There's a window above the queen-sized bed, which has a crisp, white floral print on the comforter. I sit on the bed, remembering Bri's hand on my breast and her tongue exploring my mouth.

She knocks on the doorjamb. "Here you go." She hands me the clothing.

"Thank you." I wonder how far I would have gone, if not for the phone call.

"If you need anything, I'm right down the hall. Do you want to be up by a certain time?"

"No, I'm usually up early."

"Me too. If you wake early, check my office. The next room down."

"Okay." I move to the doorway and plant a kiss on Bri, unwilling to forget the tenderness of her lips.

Bri turns on her way to her room. "I'll leave a light on in the hallway if you get up at night and need to use the bathroom."

I never thought I would have such a strong attraction for anyone again. But I believe—I *know*—these emotions are different from my feelings for Maggie. In the beginning, we shared our dreams, goals, and needs with one another, but as our relationship progressed, I realized I never felt her support. It was always about her. It took me getting burned to understand that.

I change into the tank top and shorts. They're both a little long on me, but comfortable. I walk across the hall to the bathroom, pull my hair behind my ears, lean close to the mirror, and inspect my neck.

The scars start at my left ear and go down my neck over the left side of my breast, disappearing under my tank top. I run my finger over the length of the scar on my neck. They look different now. Not as pink and purple, more like my skin tone. I touch my neck again, trying to remember how it was before. My skin will never be smooth again. I stretch my neck. The reflection tells me the laser surgery has healed. The scar is flattening, and I think it might be getting softer.

Wishful thinking. My tears build. I bend my neck from side to side and then front to back. It *seems* like I've gained more range of motion. I remind myself to do my exercises.

I was told the burn damaged some nerve endings in my skin, and they will need to regrow. And that my sense of touch may be affected. I touch my neck, then move my hand to my chest. My touch feels different between my neck and chest.

I take a deep breath, and my tears never fall.

I wonder how Bri's hand would feel if she touched the scars. Would it be different from my touch?

My eyes move to my left arm. The scar covers my arm down to the top of my hand, pitted and ridged. My hand isn't as rough, and the scar only goes to the middle of the top of my hand. The autografts did their job in replacing the burned skin. The healing process would take between one to two years to mature and change color.

It will be three years in a couple of months.

I rub my arm and chuckle as I remember what the doctor told me, *The hair on your burnt body parts may not grow back.* I skim my hand over my arm. She's right. Still no hair.

The scar is dry. Damn it, I need lotion. Should I ask Bri if I can use some of hers? I go back to the bedroom, put on my blouse, and walk down the hall. Bri's door is open a few inches. I peek into her room.

She is sitting naked on the bed, back toward me, head down. Broad shoulders. Slight love handles. Her skin contrasts between tan and white, showing a faint swimsuit line over her back. When she stands, her ass is firm, her thighs are tight, and her love handles are no longer evident.

I gasp, move from the opening, and knock. "Bri. You awake?"

"Just a minute."

When she opens the door, she's wearing a purple terry cloth robe reaching down to her knees. Her eyes roam over my body from my head to the tops of my thighs, where my blouse ends.

I clear my throat. "Do you have any lotion?"

"Ah." Her head jerks up. "Sure. It's Aveeno. Will that work?" She comes out and hands me the bottle, our hands touching.

I look down at our hands and back into her blue eyes. "Yes. Thank you."

"Anything else?"

"Yes," I grab her hand, smiling. "I wanted to ask you about the telescope, but I kind of got sidetracked." I smile.

Her hand is soft and warm. "Oh, I set it up earlier in the week and tested it for our moon gazing, but the snow clouds got in the way. So, I guess we'll have to try again." She squeezes my hand.

"I'd like that." I return the squeeze and lean in to kiss her cheek. "Thank you for a wonderful evening, despite the call."

Bri rests her forehead on mine. "Do you need anything else?"

"N-no. Good night." I turn and walk away.

"See you in the morning."

CHAPTER THIRTY-ONE

The flames. The smoke. I can't breathe. I run down a hallway, yelling for Izzy. Orange and yellow flames surround me. Thick black smoke engulfs me. I cough. I must find Izzy.

"Renata! Renata."

A gentle shake on my shoulder wakes me.

"Renata, wake up."

I jerk up and scan a darkened room, a soft ray of light shimmering from the nearby nightstand. My breathing is hard and fast. Tears are streaming down my face. I reach for the covers, but they are nowhere to be found.

"Where am I?"

"Renata, you're safe."

I turn toward the voice. Someone's silhouette is standing over the bed. "Bri?"

"You're at my house. In the spare bedroom. You're safe." She leans down and wipes my tears.

"Bri?"

She sits on the bed and touches my shoulder. "I'm here."

I fall back onto the bed and turn away from her as my tears start to fall again. The bed moves as she slowly comes behind me, covering both of us with the retrieved covers. Her body slowly spoons into mine. "You're safe. You survived."

Did I?

"Can I touch your scar on your shoulder?"

I inhale. "Yes."

She kisses my shoulder softly, then gently strokes my sweaty hair. "You're safe. I'm here."

I press back into her, grabbing her hand in mine and wrapping it around my waist. Her body engulfs me like a cocoon.

"You survived." Bri repeats, "You're safe. I'm here."

My tears stop, and I fall asleep.

CHAPTER THIRTY-TWO

When I roll onto my back the next time, it's to the aroma of bacon.

A knock at the door, and Bri's head peers around it. "Good morning, sleepyhead." Her eyes are bright.

I stretch and ask, "What time is it?"

"Nine-ish."

"Wow. I never sleep this late."

"How did you sleep?"

I sit up and take a deep breath. "I'm sorry about last night."

"Sorry about what? I heard a scream, so I came in to see if you were okay. You were curled up in a ball and crying."

I draw my knees up to my chest, embarrassed. "I didn't mean to wake you."

She comes over and sits next to me. Holding my hand, she says, "Ren, no need to be sorry. I'm glad I was here for you."

"Thank you for holding me. I fell asleep and slept the best I've slept in a long time." I squeeze her hand.

She clears her throat. "Can I ask you a question?"

"Sure."

"Oh, shit. The bacon." She jumps up and sprints out the door. "Phew, I didn't burn it. We can talk later. Breakfast first. It will be ready in ten minutes."

"Okay. I'll be there in ten."

As she leaves, I fall back onto the bed, remembering Bri telling me, *You're safe. You survived.*

The sun shines brightly through the front windows. There are no pots and pans stacked on the kitchen counter. Instead, there are two plates, a pile of bacon on each, and two glasses of orange juice.

"Wow. You cleaned up the mess from last night?"

"Yeah. I tried to be quiet—I didn't want to wake you," Bri says as she removes pancakes from a skillet onto two plates.

"I was sound asleep and didn't hear a thing."

"I'm glad." She serves me a stack of pancakes and asks, "Is two enough, or do you want three?"

"Two is fine. Thank you. It all smells delicious." I sit on the stool at the counter.

She circles around and sits next to me. "Dig in!"

Between bites, I ask, "How much snow is out there?"

"About ten inches."

"Wow."

"My neighbor down the road—Frank—plows my driveway. He hasn't been here yet."

"Friendly neighbor."

"I have good neighbors. We help each other. I helped Frank when a few of his trees came down during our last windstorm."

"What did you do?"

"I chain-sawed the limbs into manageable pieces. We stacked the wood for his fireplace."

"That sounds like a lot of hard work."

"Yep," she says, flexing her biceps. "It keeps me in shape."

"I noticed," I say shyly, heat creeping up my neck. Finally, I turn to the front window and ask, "What's that scraping sound?"

She turns. "That's probably Frank." I follow her to the front door, and freezing air swirls in when she opens it. She waves to the man in the truck plowing her driveway and yells, "Hey, Frank."

He rolls down his window. "Morning, Bri. Sure was some snowstorm last night!"

The cold makes me shiver. Bri circles my waist and pulls me close. "Thanks for plowing. I owe you a key lime pie, Frank."

"Let's get back inside. I'm cold," Bri says to me.

I stop at the counter. "Can I help clean up?"

"Nah. Not much to do. I got it. You want to take a shower?"

I do so and put on my clothing from last night without the white blouse, only my gray sweater. I find Bri thumbing through a magazine in the living room.

I sit next to her, and she turns and asks, "So, what do you want to do today?"

"Well, earlier, you were going to ask me a question before you remembered the bacon. Do you remember what it was?"

"Yeah, well, I was going to ask you if you have a lot of nightmares. But if you don't want to talk about them, that's okay."

"They come and go," I admit. "I can go for weeks and not have one. But in the past few months, I've had them more often."

"Any reason why?"

"My burnaversary is coming up."

"Burnaversary? I'm assuming that's the anniversary of the fire?"

"Yeah." I take a deep breath. "But I'd rather not talk about it right now."

"Okay. No problem." Bri puts her hand on my thigh. "What would you like to do today? It'll be a while before all the roads are clear."

"Any ideas?"

"We could watch TV, a college game. We could play a game. A Hallmark Christmas movie. I have lesbian movies, and I have a DVD set of *The Carol Burnett Show*."

I smile. "Really?"

"It's iconic! A slapstick live show? It makes you laugh out loud."

"Yeah, I remember. Let's start with that!"

Bri puts in the DVD, and we both lean back into the couch, our bodies touching from shoulder to thigh. I lean in to kiss her when she turns and points to the TV. "Watch, this scene where Carol comes down the staircase in a dress made with a curtain and the curtain rod." Carol Burnett prances down a spiral staircase in a green outfit. "It's based on Scarlett O'Hara in *Gone with the Wind*," Bri says, laughing again.

"That's hilarious! My stomach hurts from laughing."

"Mine too."

We finish watching Carol Burnett and then turn the channel to the Ohio State football game.

"This should be a good game," Bri says.

I cuddle closer to her, and she puts her arm around me. We both yell at the TV, telling a player to make a tackle or question why a player didn't catch a pass. Eventually, my head is on Bri's lap and her hand on my hip.

The next thing I know, I hear a snorting noise. I sit up to see Bri's head resting on the back of the couch, her mouth slightly open, snoring. I chuckle.

Her slight belly fat hangs over the top of her jeans. She's wearing a ragged terry cloth pullover with frayed cuffs, her hands folded on her stomach. I run my hands over a sleeve. It is soft, like it's been washed over a hundred times.

My eyes take in her muscular legs and feet resting on the ottoman. I read her socks: *More Feminism, Less Bullshit*.

She was so caring last night, so gentle. She didn't ask for any explanations. She said she would wait.

She held me. I felt safe.

I rub the back of my hand over her cheek. "Bri, I think I'm falling for you," I whisper to myself.

CHAPTER THIRTY-THREE

"Wasn't Saturday night's snowstorm beautiful?" Darlene says as we walk into her house after attending the boys' Monday night basketball game.

I drop my coat onto the sofa. "I know. The snow was really beautiful."

"How long did it take for the city to clear your street?"

"Um…not sure."

Darlene opens the refrigerator and asks, "You want some water?"

"Yes, please."

She grabs two bottles of water and hands me one as we both move onto the couch. "Wait a minute. What do you mean, you're not sure?"

My face begins to heat up.

Darlene turns toward me and grabs my arm. "Tell me."

"Tell you what?"

"Your eyes are telling me something happened."

"They are?"

"Yes." Darlene slaps the couch. "Spill it."

"Okay." I grin. "I stayed at Bri's Saturday night."

"What?"

"She invited me over to dinner."

"Then what?"

"Well, the snow kept falling. Driving home would be dangerous, so I spent the night."

"Yeah…"

I roll my eyes. "In her spare bedroom."

Darlene's shoulders slump. "Darn. I was hoping for more."

"Depends on what you mean by more."

"Come on, more…you know, sex?"

"No sex. But we did cuddle and kiss."

"Woohoo! Ms. Santos is back in the saddle!" Darlene moves her arm above her head like she's twirling a lasso, making me laugh. "I'm happy for you! You deserve to be happy. You've been through so much. I want you to find happiness again."

"Thank you. I'm still—I need more time."

"And?"

"Bri is willing to go slow."

CHAPTER THIRTY-FOUR

I'm at home on the couch, working Tuesday evening, when my phone rings.

Bri's ringtone. My heart races. A FaceTime call.

When I answer, a sheepish smile and blue eyes appear on the screen. "Hi, Bri!"

"Ren. Busy?"

"Nah. Working on budget revisions. Just got done with dinner." I comb my fingers through my hair.

"You're beautiful."

I blush. "Stop, you're embarrassing me. What's up?"

Bri stares at her phone. "Sorry, I have another call. It's my brother. Can you hold?"

"Sure, go ahead. I'll be here."

"Thanks."

Bri disappears. A few minutes later, her smiling face reappears.

"I'm back."

"Everything okay?"

"Yeah. David got a promotion at work. He's waited a long time for this and has worked hard. And it's paid off! He's advancing to the CFO position at his company in Cincinnati."

"That's wonderful!"

"Yeah. I'm so happy for him. We set up a day to meet and talk more about it."

"So what's up?"

"Well, I'm wondering whether it would be okay to stop by your house sometime this week after work. I want to share some news with you, but I want to do it in person."

I'm instantly nervous. "Sounds…interesting."

"What would be a good night?"

"How about Wednesday?"

"Sorry, I'm meeting David and Liz to celebrate his promotion."

"Okay, so…Thursday?"

"Sure, that works for me."

"Can I ask why you used FaceTime to call me?"

"I—I wanted to see you," Bri says, looking shy. "I wanted to tell you I had a wonderful time this weekend, and I hope we can do it again…soon."

"So do I."

"I'm happy you want to spend time with me again," she says, clearing her throat. "I'll let you return to your budget. I have paperwork to complete tonight too."

"I'm looking forward to Thursday."

We wave goodbye and end the call.

CHAPTER THIRTY-FIVE

I sit in the restaurant's waiting area, thinking about Bri, and finally bring myself back to reality as Clare walks in. "Over here!" I smile widely as Clare engulfs me in a hug. "Thanks, sis, for meeting for an early dinner. I know Wednesdays work best for you."

"No problem. I'm always glad to see my big sister. And you did pick Olive Garden, so how can I resist?" Clare jokes as the hostess leads us to our table. We maneuver between tables of couples and families, dodging servers carrying trays of food.

As we take our places at a table in the corner, the hostess takes our drink order, and we catch up about Izzy getting ready for Halloween.

Clare gives me a look. "Okay, so now, you had this huge smile on when I walked in. What's going on with you?"

I take a deep breath. "I stayed at Bri's this past weekend."

"Oh?"

"But before that, I want to tell you something. I've been getting anonymous phone calls from some guy."

We're interrupted by the delivery of our drinks and the server asking for our food order.

"Ren, when did this start?" Clare asks, looking horrified.

"A month or so. I thought it was nothing, so I didn't say anything."

"But now?"

"I received some flowers, and I thought they were from Bri, but they weren't. And yesterday I got more with a card that said, 'I hope you like the flowers and I hope to see you soon.'"

"Holy shit, Ren." She looks aghast now. "You need to call the police."

"I did. Bri convinced me to call the other night. I talked with an officer—a woman, thank God. Her name is Abby Jackson. She took the report over the phone since it was the night of the snowstorm. She asked about my home security, and I told her I have a monitored back-to-base system and a doorbell camera."

"Did she say they could do anything?"

"She stopped by yesterday morning before I headed to school and got the card that came with the flowers since it has the flower shop's name on it. She's going to contact the store and see if there's a video or if she can gather other information from the employees."

"Did you get her contact information?"

"I have her card, and she told me to call her if anything else happens."

"Well, I guess that's something? You okay with that?"

I swallow nervously. "For now."

Clare grabs my hand. "You sure? You can always call Ryan or me if you need anything. We're only fifteen minutes away."

"Thanks, but I'm okay for now."

"If you're sure."

"Yeah, I'm sure."

"So, back to you staying at Bri's?" She leans toward me, grinning.

"Stop." I hold out my hands, palms up. "Because of the snowstorm, I couldn't drive home."

"Oh. Good excuse."

"No, really, that was the reason," I laugh. "But—"

"But?" Our salad, cheese dip and breadsticks arrive, and Clare adds, "Hold that thought."

Cheese grinder in hand, the server asks, "How much cheese?"

She grinds and grinds, and I say, "Clare, there's going to be more cheese than salad."

Finally, my sister waves her hand and says, "Thanks, that's enough."

"Okay," Clare says, "back to the but—"

"But I think I'm falling for her."

Her eyes light up, "Oh, Ren! I'm so happy for you. You know Izzy keeps asking when Bri is coming back to play football."

"I enjoyed the game—and the laughter. And how Bri handled Ash's—I don't know, her confrontation. It helped me open up." I take a drink of water. "It was a fun afternoon. And Bri had a good time too."

"You gonna eat the rest of the breadsticks?"

"No, go ahead."

She smothers them in the cheese dip. "They make the best breadsticks. Sorry. Back to Bri."

I lower my head. "She saw some of my scarring."

"And?"

"She asked to touch the scar on my shoulder."

"And?"

"I'm very nervous about the…next step…of our relationship."

Clare reaches over and covers her hand over mine. "What are you nervous about?"

She knows where I'm headed, but I appreciate her letting me say it.

"Sex," I say, a little too loudly.

In a lower voice, she says, "You're concerned about making love?"

I nod quickly.

"Are you ready for that?"

"Bri told me we could go slow. And that she'll follow my lead."

"That's a good thing, right?"

"Yes, but—what will she think when she sees the scars on the rest of my body?"

"Ren."

"Will she want to touch me? Will she run? Will she leave me?"

"You mean like Maggie did?"

I sigh. "I'm not sure I'm ready to show the scars to anyone yet."

"Bri said she would wait. Did she pressure you over the weekend?"

"No. She didn't. She was very understanding and—"

"And?"

"I feel safe with her. Comfortable."

"That's a beginning."

Suddenly, I hear a voice I recognize. I watch Bri walk in with a woman, her back to me as a server leads them to a table in the opposite corner.

"Ren, are you okay? Your face is white as a ghost." She follows my eyes. "Oh my God, is that Bri?"

I watch as Bri releases the woman from a hug and sits with her back to me. What the hell? I thought she was meeting with her brother and sister-in-law in Cincinnati today. I stare at the woman. Look at her with her long blond hair pulled back behind her ear, revealing dangly earrings. Her midi dress displays athletic legs—and plump and perky breasts.

I vaguely hear Clare say something about not jumping to conclusions. Blood rushes in my ears as I tell myself that hug lasted longer than a "nice to see you again."

"Ren." Clare grabs my hands.

I look at Bri and back to the woman. How I compete with that? My breath starts to change.

"Ren. Calm down. Deep breaths."

Why would she lie to me?

I can't think straight. I take a few deep breaths. Then, finally, I stand, "I have to leave, sis. I'm sorry." I throw on my coat and walk toward the door.

"Ren, wait for me."

Clare throws money on the table. We leave, making sure Bri doesn't see us.

CHAPTER THIRTY-SIX

The next evening, I pace in my house as I wait for Bri to arrive. I should call her and cancel. The anonymous caller scares me. What if he does something to her if he finds out I'm with her? And then seeing Bri with another woman... It's making me wary of everything.

A knock at the door. I recall Clare's advice. *Don't jump to conclusions. Ask her. Talk with her.*

Bri's cheeks are rosy and her eyes tear up from the cold. "Hi, Ren." As she leans in to kiss me I turn my face so she kisses my cheek. She leans back, scrutinizing me, tilting her head.

"Come in. You're shivering."

She walks past me, carrying a bottle. "I have some awesome news," she says as she takes off her coat and hustles into the kitchen. "Where is the wine opener?"

"In the drawer to your left."

Why is she acting like there's nothing wrong? She was with another woman. Does she think I'd jump into bed with the first person who showed me some attention?

She finds the corkscrew, puts the bottle on the counter, and continues, "The company accepted the acquisition terms! We are so excited. This is going to be great for both companies and all employees, financially and professionally. I was thinking you and I could go to New York City to some Broadway plays to celebrate. You said you've never been."

When I don't respond, Bri lifts her head and studies me. She stops extracting the cork.

"Renata, is something wrong? You haven't said a word since I walked in."

I walk past her. Her eyes follow me. I go into the bathroom, take off all my clothes, and put on my long robe. I come back into the kitchen.

Bri sets the bottle of wine down. Her eyes run up and down my body.

"Why don't we jump to the celebration you came for," I say flatly. Isn't that why she's here? To compare me to her date?

"What are you talking about?"

"Isn't this what you hoped would happen?"

"No!" Bri shakes her head, confusion written all over her face.

I snort. "Why? Did you already fuck your date from yesterday?"

"Ren." Bri's jaw tenses and wrinkles appear between her eyebrows. "You are not making any sense. I didn't have a date yesterday."

"I saw you at Olive Garden with a blonde. You hugged her."

"Ren. Stop." She takes a step toward me.

"I thought you were going to meet David and Liz?"

"I am so confused." She shakes her head multiple times and takes a deep breath. "What are you talking about?"

Why am I so outraged? I don't even know who the blonde is and why she was with Bri. I raise my hands. "I'm sorry. Give me a minute."

I turn and go into my bedroom and sit, my hands on the bed steadying me. What am I doing? Bri has always been kind and understanding. I inhale and exhale. I need to explain how I'm feeling. I change back into my clothes and return to the kitchen.

"Please forgive me. I don't know why I reacted that way. You don't deserve that."

Her brow furrows. "You're right. I don't."

"Can we sit and talk?"

"Why?"

"Because I actually might have an idea as to why I reacted so cruelly to you." We sit on the couch and I grab her hand. "Seeing you with that woman just made me—I don't know, my mind went down the rabbit hole of self-doubt."

"Renata—"

"No, let me finish. I was going to show my scars to you to see if you would turn and run like Maggie did." I touch her hand. "But you're not Maggie, and I need to start trusting you."

"Renata, you are beautiful, inside and out."

I look at Bri.

"Inside. Your heart is the best part of you," Bri says as she places her hand over my heart. "That's what attracts me to you. That's what I want to touch. Outside…your scars are part of you. They reflect your bravery and courage in the battle you fought—the battle you survived."

"But these scars"—I point to them, hidden under my shirt—"remind me of the body and the love I lost."

"I am attracted to you," she says, "but you need to let me in—into your heart."

Tears flood my eyes. "Bri, I'm not sure how. Please be patient with me," I beg as a tear falls down my cheek. "I'm also scared the anonymous phone caller will do something to you. I think his calls and my seeing you are connected somehow."

Bri stares at me. "Renata, nothing is going to happen to me. But if the person contacts me or anything fishy happens, I'm calling Sergeant Jackson."

"You will?"

"Of course. You said some pretty hurtful things to me." She runs her hand through her hair. "And I need some time to process what happened tonight. So I think I'll be going."

"I'm sorry."

"I know. You say that quite a bit."

Her words grow legs, kicking me hard. I nod slowly as Bri puts on her coat.

"Thanks for talking with me about how you're feeling. I appreciate it. But I don't know if I can do this emotional roller-coaster ride with you right now."

"Bri?"

When she reaches the door, she turns, looks me in the eye, and says, "It's up to you what happens next." Then she opens the door and walks out.

I stare at the door. She didn't even explain about the blonde.

CHAPTER THIRTY-SEVEN

"What the fuck am I doing?" I say out loud.

There is no way I could go to work today, so I took a personal day and called Clare to ask if she could drop by after work. So here we sit side by side in the middle of my couch.

"What happened? The dark circles under your eyes tell me you haven't been sleeping well. You need your rest."

"No shit. Don't lecture me. You're not my mother," I snap.

Clare moves to the end of the couch and says calmly, "So, why did you call me? Why am I here?"

I stand. I sit. I put my hands on my thighs. "I think I'm falling in love with Bri."

She raises her eyebrows coolly. "So why aren't you jumping up and down?"

"I fucked up."

"Meaning?"

"Meaning, she came in, and I didn't even ask her about the other woman. I couldn't stop my mind from going down the dark hole of—"

"Of being the victim?" Clare interrupts.

"Yes, poor me," I say bitterly. "A burn victim. Lover walks out on me, victim." My hands cover my face. "Luckily, I came to my senses, which hasn't happened in a while, and I apologized once I realized I was acting like an ass."

"Did you ask her about the woman?"

"No, she left so quickly, I didn't get a chance."

"Have you thought about going back to the Phoenix virtual support group? Or the peer-support chat?"

"What, so they can tell me how lucky I am because the fire burned only thirty percent of my body?"

"Ren."

I sigh. "I know…the group members are not the problem. I feel guilty because of others whose burns are worse than mine. I'm embarrassed to complain or talk about my issues."

"Remember when we joined together? We learned a change in appearance might impact women more than men."

"Really?" I stand and raise my voice. "Of course, society bombards women with subliminal messages about how a woman must be sexy with a beautiful body."

"Ren, please."

I inhale and walk away from Clare. "Bri said I'm brave and courageous and that my scars are the results of a battle I survived."

"Remember what Izzy said when we played football?"

"No."

"She said you were the best survivor." Clare moves closer to me and touches my arm. "Ren, everyone thinks you're a survivor except you."

I lower my head and voice. "I know."

"You integrated back into the work environment and the public."

"Not fully. I still cover up the scars on my ear and neck."

"But it doesn't stop you from going out in public. One step at a time. It's only been—or soon will be—three years."

I think back. "It wasn't easy to go back with all the students and staff staring. I could see their brains working, asking themselves how damaged I was, whether I could still do my job."

"So, is this more about what we talked about at lunch? The sexual part of the relationship?"

"Maybe."

"Phoenix did say your libido may be affected."

"Well, I thought it was for a while, but believe me, it's back in action." I remember how my body reacted when Bri kissed and touched me.

"Let's back up. Tell me what happened?"

I explain with details about last night: how I almost showed Bri my scars, how we talked about my fear of something happening to her because this male phone stalker knows about her, and my reluctance to let her into my heart.

"So a woman who expressed her feelings for you honored your request to go slow. Right?"

"Yes."

"A woman who makes you laugh and embraces and calms you after a nightmare."

I turn away from Clare. "Ugh. Yes."

"You pushed her away—with, may I say, a damn hard push."

"I—it's—I don't know if I can survive the rejection."

"Rejection of what? Your body? She hasn't seen your body, so I don't think that's the issue, do you?"

"Clare—"

"Look at me."

I turn and face her, and she says, "You still see yourself as a victim. Until you can move past that, I don't think you'll let anyone touch you. And I mean figuratively *and* emotionally."

"But—"

"But nothing. It's up to you where you go with Bri from here."

CHAPTER THIRTY-EIGHT

Saturday morning, I decide to go to a nearby park for a walk after breakfast. The cold air hits my face, and I pull down my sock cap over my ears. I stick my gloved hands in my Cargill jacket and kick a small tree limb off the macadam path with my snow boots.

Geese are floating in the half-frozen pond to the right, and the trees lining the walkway have birds taking in the early sunbeams as I walk and ponder the last couple of months. I think of Bri commenting on how I'm always saying I'm sorry and Clare saying I act like a victim.

I thought I'd dealt with all of this in therapy, so why is everything coming back now? And who is the man calling me, and what does he want? Maybe it's because my burnaversary is coming up. Perhaps I met this man in a support group.

I've got to do something if I want to move forward with my life. I need to face my fears and get back into the group because I don't want to lose Bri—not that I ever had her, or that she'll even talk to me.

I should have gone back to the group as soon as the dreams started again.

Back home, I look up the Phoenix Society for Burn Survivors and to find a meeting tonight.

"I need to do something for me," I say to the faces of the nine group members on the virtual Zoom meeting. "Someone in my life cares for me, and I want to let them in. But I keep throwing up roadblocks."

"What's causing the derailment?" a group member asks.

"I still view myself as a...victim."

"Tell us your story. We're here for you," another group member encourages.

CHAPTER THIRTY-NINE

At Thanksgiving dinner, Clare asked about Bri. I told her I hadn't heard from her but that I was attending the support groups again. She hugged me and said she was proud of me.

I miss Bri. I wonder what she did for Thanksgiving. Did she spend it with her brother and sister-in-law or her coworkers? Should I call her? Maybe send a short text wishing her Happy Thanksgiving. I wonder if she's wearing socks with Thanksgiving turkeys.

The following week, I stop on my way to work to pick up donuts for the teachers' lounge. As I walk into the shop, I stop and stare.

Bri is pulling her credit card out of the machine and grabbing a box of donuts from the cashier. She walks my way and comes to a halt as our eyes meet. "Good morning, Renata."

I step out of line and say, "Morning, Bri."

We stand and stare at each other.

I quickly say, "How are you?"

"I'm doing okay. Picking up some donuts to take to work."
She looks at her watch. "Speaking of, I need to go. We have a
meeting this morning."

"Okay." I step aside and let her pass. I have to say more. I
can't just let her walk out without saying something. I follow her
out the door and yell, "Bri!"

She turns. "Yeah?"

"Can we talk?" Please say yes.

My stomach drops when she shakes her head. "I'm not
ready yet. I have the acquisition to deal with and my bro—never
mind." She shakes her head. "No, I need some more time. And
I need to get going."

I step away from her car as she gets in. "It's good to see you,"
I say too late.

I'm no longer interested in donuts, so I head to my car. I
get an eerie feeling, my hair on my neck bristling like someone
is watching me. I tell myself it's the cold—or the cold shoulder
from Bri.

CHAPTER FORTY

The following week, I attend my fifth group meeting, highlighting my progress over the past soon-to-be three years.

A member says, "You dealt with the depression, but anxiety will always be with there for some of us, and that's okay. We learn to deal with it."

"I guess it's just my body image," I say.

"Bullshit!" another says. She's in her late twenties, with scars covering most of her face.

"What do you mean, bullshit?" I ask, leaning toward my computer screen.

"For you, your scars represent your asshole of an ex-girlfriend's rejection of your body, not you."

"What do you mean?"

"You see me, right? Well, sixty percent of my body was burnt. Anyone who wants to be with me accepts this body, scars and all. Why? Because they're a part of me. I went to hell and back, as did most of us."

Another member shouts, "You go, girl!"

"That hell made me stronger. That hell tells me I can handle anything. And fuck anyone who doesn't acknowledge the beauty beneath the scars, because, baby"—she points at herself—"I'm beautiful, through and through." Then she points at me. "And so are you."

"Yeah. So what are you gonna do about it, beautiful?" another member asks.

CHAPTER FORTY-ONE

On Friday night I reach for my phone and dial Bri's number. If she doesn't want to see me, I at least need to tell her the anonymous caller mentioned the other woman again.

She answers on the fourth ring. "Hello?"

"Bri. It's Ren."

"Yeah, your name shows on the screen. I wasn't sure I wanted to answer."

"I—ah—would not blame you if you didn't."

"Why are you calling?"

I bite my lip. "I wanted to apologize. I said some hurtful things to you, and I'm sorry."

"Yes. You did."

"I want to explain."

Silence. Then, "Ren, I'm confused. I thought we were moving in the right direction, getting to know each other, then you—I don't know. Your appalling accusations—"

"I know. I know. Please let me explain."

Silence. "I'll give you five minutes."

"My sister and I were at Olive Garden, and you were with another woman. An attractive woman, I might say. You hugged her for a long time, but you told me just the night before you were meeting with your brother."

"Yes. I met David and Liz for lunch. The woman was my ex, Olivia. Her father died a few months back, and he has property here in town. She was here to handle some legal matters with the estate. I wanted to offer her my condolences and catch up."

I lean my head on my hand. I need to explain things to her. "I-I made assumptions and jumped to the conclusion that—"

"Yes, you did."

"I should have asked you about her."

"Right, you should have." Her voice is tense. "But then you couldn't use it as an excuse to push me away, could you?"

She's right. "Bri, I want to see you again."

"I'm not sure." Her voice is flat.

"I'm doing some serious thinking and processing…with the help of some friends. I would like to share some of what I've been doing. How I'm moving forward."

"I don't know. I started to believe I might have a chance at love again. But I don't know. This all seems too hard, and I'm not sure I want to be hurt again."

I tilt my head. Did I just hear what I thought I heard? Did she say *a chance at love again*? A chunk of the wall around my heart disintegrates.

I need to figure out a way to spend time with her and tell my story. "Could we meet somewhere, maybe for coffee or a drink?"

"I—"

"You told me we could go slow."

"Yeah, I remember."

"I needed a rest stop to determine why I took a detour leading to a dead end."

"Yeah. A dead end that came out of nowhere for me. Your accusation…I felt like I walked off the edge of a cliff."

"I know. I'm sorry, and I want to share with you the map of how I got to the dead end and how I want to move forward."

"I need more time—"

I don't want to push her away. I'll give her the time she needs. "Okay. I respect that. And it might be a good idea anyway."

"What do you mean?"

"The other reason I called was to tell you I reported another incident to Sergeant Jackson about that man calling me."

"He contacted you again?" I hear her concern.

"Yes. He told me he saw me with a woman and she better stay away from me."

A pause. "Ren, this is getting serious."

"Yeah, so maybe it's better we take a break from seeing each other. I don't want anything to happen to you because of me, and it will give you the time you need to figure out what you need to figure out."

"Renata—"

"I'll be fine. Sergeant Jackson said if he contacts you or anything suspicious happens, you need to contact her." I pause. "Bri, promise me you will."

"I promise. And you promise to watch your back. I don't want anything to happen to you before"—I hear a chuckle— "before I figure out you and me."

I squeeze my eyes and exhale. "Okay. I'll let you go."

"Thanks for calling."

CHAPTER FORTY-TWO

I stand in Darlene's kitchen Saturday night, watching her add something to her spaghetti sauce that she shields from view. I inhale the comforting, delicious aroma, my mouth watering.

"Are you ever going to share that secret ingredient?" I ask.

As she stirs the sauce, she says dramatically, her hand over her heart, "Never."

"You give me the same answer every time."

We laugh. She turns and takes a spoonful of sauce into her mouth. She licks her lips. "Family secret."

"By the way, I'm glad you invited me for dinner. I need a change in scenery."

Darlene looks at me. "What's going on with you, my friend?"

"What do you mean?"

"Well, you asked me to run the department head meeting and to observe two disciplinary meetings this week."

"Yeah. You did tell me you want to eventually become a principal one day. I thought I'd let you get a taste of some of the responsibilities." Darlene looks at me sheepishly. "What's going on with you? Something on your mind?"

"Yeah." Darlene drops the spoon on the counter. "You're right. I do want to become a principal, and a friend who works at Valley View High School said her vice principal is retiring at the end of this school year. I think that would be the next logical step."

"And are you going to apply?"

"You think I should?"

I grab Darlene by her shoulders and shake her. "Absolutely, girlfriend. You are ready."

Darlene steps away, standing tall. "I am ready. Thanks to you."

"Look, this has always been your goal. You have teaching experience, department head experience, curriculum director experience…You're ready."

Darlene hugs me. "I'm ready."

"And I'll be your first reference."

"Thanks, Renata."

"Oh, I'm so happy for you! And at the same time, I'll miss you."

"Stop—the job hasn't even been posted. Who knows, the vice principal may change their mind."

"Doesn't matter. If not Valley View, it will be another school."

"I hope so." She picks up the spoon, turns back to the stove and says, "So I've noticed you've been holed up in your office more than usual. What's going on?"

I lean against the island. "Preoccupied."

"What are you thinking about? You're staring a hole through the bottle of wine on the counter. Do you want some?"

"Yeah, I think I do." I pick up the bottle. "Merlot. Excellent choice."

"So, what are you thinking?" Darlene asks as I pour us both a drink.

"About us and how we met and how our friendship developed." I smile. "And how lucky I am to call you my friend."

Darlene finishes dropping the spaghetti into the boiling water and turns, confusion on her face. "Where is all this coming from?"

"I'm not sure," I say, twisting the glass in my hands.

Darlene wipes her hands on a towel and stands across from me at the counter. She reaches for her glass and takes a sip. "Does this have anything to do with Bri?"

"Maybe."

"Spill, and I don't mean the wine."

I chuckle. "Good one, but not tonight. It's just…you had my back when that math teacher made accusations about my sexuality and inherent bias when I didn't renew his contract." I grab her hand. "And when I needed someone during my recovery and when Maggie left me, you were there."

Darlene's eyes fill with tears. "You would do the same for me. We climbed up the mountain and back down together. Remember, you were by my side when Nancy broke up with me. You guided me through my master's and went to bat for me for the curriculum director job. Tell me what's on your mind."

I look at the stove and point. "What about the spaghetti?"

"Oh, shit." Darlene turns to the stove. "Yeah. It should be almost ready."

A few minutes later, she drains the spaghetti and dumps it into a large bowl. "Ready. Can you get the salad and dressing out of the refrigerator?"

"Got it."

Darlene adds, "Oh, and the bread in the oven?"

"Sure. It smells wonderful, as usual," I say. I find hot pads and open the oven, and when the heat pours out onto my arms, I freeze. But I don't react negatively to the heat as I did in the past. I smile and retrieve the bread.

"Dig in," Darlene says.

I take a forkful and hum. "This is delicious."

"So…tell me, what's up?"

"Oh, I fucked up big time with Bri." I take a deep breath. "But I'm hoping we can talk soon so I can explain everything to her and return to where we were before I blew it. She's been supportive and understanding of my journey—which is what I'm calling it now—to try to make sense of how the scars impact me and my assumptions."

"Didn't you tell me you discussed all that during individual therapy?" Darlene asks as she takes a forkful of salad.

"Yeah, but I guess, at that time, I wasn't ready to—or just didn't—believe the scars and Maggie's rejection were related to my assumptions."

"Maybe you have a reason now to see the connection."

"Yeah, it's becoming very clear."

"Back to you wanting to explain to Bri."

"Yeah." I push my spaghetti around my plate with my fork. "I want to tell her why I did what I did and said. What I said, all of which was inappropriate and stupid and hurtful and—"

"Okay," Darlene says, waving her fork, "I get it."

"And I want to make sure she's safe. And I want to tell her I care about her." I drop my fork onto my plate, and spaghetti sauce splashes onto my white blouse. "Oh, damn." I grab my napkin, dip it in my water glass, and gingerly dab the sauce spots.

"Use some Shout on it when you wash it. That should take care of it."

I slump in my chair. "I care about her. I care a lot."

"Then you need to tell her."

"But she's upset with me right now, probably more than upset. So do I wait, or do I stop by this weekend?"

"What could it hurt to stop by?"

"I don't know. If I stop and a car is in the driveway, I can always turn around and leave."

"Your call. I think Bri is a reasonable person."

"True. I know I'm part of the problem, but—"

"You care about her?"

"Yes. So, what do I do?"

"Do what you always tell me. Follow your gut. What's your gut saying?"

I close my eyes and then open them. "It says to stop by."

CHAPTER FORTY-THREE

On Sunday afternoon, I drive across the bike path as the snow begins to fall. As I turn into Bri's driveway, I look at the month-to-month guide to stargazing sitting in the passenger seat. My fingers are wrapped so tightly around the steering wheel, my hands hurt. There are no cars in sight. I breathe a sigh of relief.

As I walk to the front door, holding the book, I raise my hand to knock on the door. Then I freeze.

I had practiced what I want to say on my way here, but it changed every time. It went from apologizing again for my behavior to how I can support her in dealing with her brother's situation to telling her I'm falling in love with her.

Am I falling in love with her?

I cover my face with my free hand and shake my head. I should not be here. I drop my hand, and as I turn to leave, my eyes catch a movement to the right of me, toward the bike path.

A man appears—tall, broad-shouldered, wearing a brown, knee-length duffel coat, dark pants and black boots. His hands are in his coat pockets, and his hood is over his head. My eyes follow him as he turns into Bri's yard. Should I be scared? Who is this person?

He glances at the house and stops when he sees me standing on the porch. He lowers his hood and starts walking closer.

I feel my heart start to pound. He continues until he steps onto the porch, and our eyes meet. His eyes are the same color as Bri's.

"Renata?"

Oh. Relief washes over me. "Hi, David."

"So, Renata." He looks me up and down. "I've heard you and Bri are not seeing each other anymore."

This is not going as planned. What did Bri tell him? Does he know what I did and said? *Stay strong*, I tell myself. It doesn't matter what he knows about me. I'm here to visit Bri.

"I thought I'd stop by. Is she home?"

"I'm not sure this is a good time."

The door swings open, and someone says, "David, we were getting worried." Liz, in blue jeans and a heavy red sweater, stands behind the half-opened door, staring at me. "Renata! Where did you come from?"

"She was standing on the porch. She's here to see Bri."

"Oh." She glances back into the house and then back to me. No one says a word as we stare at each other.

"Bri," Liz yells back into the house, "someone is here to see you."

"I'm not expecting anyone. Who the hell is it?" Bri says as she arrives at the half-opened door. Then she stops in her tracks. "Renata. I thought you were going to give me time to figure us out?"

I look at David and Liz, my eyebrows raised, hoping to send them a message to go inside so I can talk to Bri. They don't budge.

My teeth start to chatter as I wrap my arms around myself. I didn't dress thinking I'd be stuck outside in the cold. "I didn't think you had company. I didn't see a car in the driveway."

"We parked in the garage," David says.

"Oh."

Bri looks to David and Liz and says, "Come in. You're shivering."

Her eyes meet David's. Finally, he moves aside. Liz closes the door behind us and says, "I'll make coffee and hot chocolate. Which do you prefer, Renata?"

"Um, hot chocolate, please."

"Same for me," David says as he takes off his coat and hangs it on the coat rack. He turns, his eyes darting from me to Bri, telling me, *Be careful, I'm watching you.* He heads toward the kitchen.

Bri and I stand in the entryway, facing each other. "What are you doing here?" she asks again.

"I wanted to drop off this book I thought you would like." I put my hand on her arm. "And I want to thank you for your support and understanding."

She moves her arm out from under my hand. "Not sure my support of you got us anywhere."

"I guess I better go then." And I turn to go back to my car.

A hand touches my shoulder. "Stop."

I don't turn around. The warmth of her touch radiates through my coat.

"Renata."

Finally, I turn to face her. "Here." And I shove the book at her.

Bri takes it and reads the title. "Why?"

"Because I wanted to do something for you to show you I care." I turn back toward the door.

"Renata? Give me your coat and stay until you warm up."

"I don't want to intrude."

"You need to warm up. Come into the living room. I'll get your hot chocolate."

CHAPTER FORTY-FOUR

Sitting on the couch where Bri and I first made out, I remember how she was respectful, patient, and gentle toward me, my body, and my feelings.

"Your hot chocolate," Bri says, her voice only slightly thawed.

When I grab the cup, our fingers touch, sending electricity through my body. "Thank you."

David leans against the kitchen counter as Liz sits on the other end of the couch and Bri sits on the high-back chair. No one says anything as we all sip our hot drinks.

I search Bri's face for some sign of anger, confusion, hurt, sadness—anything. She looks painfully neutral.

Finally, she turns to David. "How was your walk?"

"It helped me clear my head."

"Why don't you come to sit by me?" Liz asks.

"Nah. I'll stand," David answers.

Silence falls again, except for the *ticktock* of the grandmother clock.

Liz breaks the silence. "Renata, how have you been since we last saw you?"

"Busy, as usual."

"Working with high school kids must be challenging," she presses.

"It can be, I guess. For me, I enjoy working with young people. Now, if you're talking about junior high students, that's a different story."

"From what I saw in her interactions with the staff when our team visited the school, Renata is well-respected by the students and staff," Bri adds.

I nod gratefully in her direction.

Tick. Tock. Tick. Tock.

Silence.

Tick. Tock.

I move from the couch toward the door. "Obviously"—I make eye contact with all three of them—"I am intruding and need to go. I'm sorry for showing up unannounced. Please forgive me." I can't move quickly enough.

"One thing before you leave," David says. "I need to share something with you."

Bri comes and stands between David and me.

"Okay."

"The night we had dinner I could tell my sister was happy. And from what she told me, you make her happy. But lately, she hasn't been herself. And I was wondering if that has something to do with you?"

"David, this is between Renata and me," Bri interrupts.

"I know, sis, but like I said, seeing you two together at dinner, the way you smiled and blushed." His eyes meet Bri's then mine, and then back to Bri. "Don't give up on each other. Liz, can you come here, please?" David reaches out his hand and gestures for his wife to join us. He takes a deep breath. "And while we're all here, I want to say, I know I've resisted returning to AA. I called my old sponsor on my walk, and he recommended another sponsor. I promised him I would return to the meetings." He looks between Bri and Liz. "And I promise the both of you I will return."

Liz hugs her husband.

"Thank you both for your support and"—he punches Bri's shoulder—"not giving up on me."

I take a step backward toward the door as Bri hugs them both.

I grab my coat, open the door and throw one last glance in Bri's direction, just in time to see tears running down her cheeks as she says to David, "I love you."

"I love you too, sis."

I walk to my car and stop to gaze up into the sky. I barely see the new moon but the planets shine bright. And as the new moon is known as a time to initiate new beginnings, I smile. I'm happy for Bri and her brother. It seems he's back on track. Now I can only hope there's a new beginning ahead for me.

CHAPTER FORTY-FIVE

The following week is full of school activities and end-of-semester paperwork. One night after school, Darlene and I meet at El Cazador for dinner to discuss the VR project. Darlene has an interview for the vice principal position at Valley View High, so she wants to pick my brains about possible interview questions too.

"We're done eating, so how about one final question?" she says.

"Okay, let me think of another one." I ponder for a moment. "Describe a time when a situation needed to be handled with sensitivity and tact. What was the issue, how did you deal with it, and what was the outcome?"

"Well—"

Suddenly, someone is standing next to our table. I jump in my seat, and the person says, "Sorry, I didn't mean to scare you."

I look up to see our board president. "Mr. Fisher!" I exhale in relief. I am still getting anonymous calls despite my reporting each and every one to the police. "No problem. You just startled me, but it's nice to see you."

"Hello, Renata—Darlene."

"Bob, good to see you," Darlene says.

"Sorry to interrupt your dinner. When I saw you, I wanted to stop by and ask you, Renata, if you would be able to stop by the board office tomorrow. I have some questions related to the VR proposal."

I look to Darlene and then up to Bob. "Sure."

"I'll be in the office around two. Could you make it then?"

"Of course. I'll see you tomorrow."

"Good—thank you. Enjoy your dinner."

Darlene and I watch him pay his bill and leave the restaurant.

"What was that?" I ask. "The only time I see him is at the board meetings or fundraisers."

"And I wonder what more he wants to know about the VR proposal," Darlene muses.

"I'm still working on the budget."

"I hope it's nothing that's going to jeopardize our final proposal and presentation?"

I raise my hand to get the server. "Oh, don't worry. He probably has questions about the background information we presented at the last meeting now that he's had time to do some research of his own."

Checking my phone as I slide out of the booth, I see I have a voice message. I had my ring on silent so it may be Bri. I go to my voice message and listen.

"Hello, Renata," a man's voice says. "I see you are now with yet another woman."

I collapse back into the booth, my eyes frantically roaming around the restaurant, looking for a man on a phone. Darlene grabs my arm. "Ren, what's wrong?"

I hold my phone to my chest. "It's him," I hiss, "and he said he sees me with another woman."

Darlene scans the room, still holding my arm. Neither of us sees anything as I return to my seat.

"This is scaring me now," Darlene says.

I take a deep breath and dial Sergeant Jackson.

CHAPTER FORTY-SIX

When I arrive home, I consider calling Bri to tell her about the latest call. It doesn't matter if we continue to see each other—what's important is that she's safe.

I laugh to myself. Who am I trying to kid? It does matter. I want to see her again.

She answers on the second ring. "Hello, Renata."

I jump right in. "I'm not sure you want to hear from me, but I wanted to tell you I had another call from my stalker."

"Jesus, Ren. Did you call the sergeant?"

I tell her about the call and my conversation with Sergeant Jackson, then say, "I think...it's best we not see each other for a while."

A pause. "Look, Renata. I've been thinking about us and don't like this guy calling you. And...I want to be there for you." Silence. She continues, "But we need to talk first."

I try to contain the giddy grin spreading across my face. "Okay. How about I make you dinner this weekend?"

"Ah—"

Silence again. Have I given her enough rope to pull her back up, or have I pushed her over the edge again?

Please say yes.

"Yes."

"So you'll come to dinner?"

"I guess so, but not this weekend. But the following one is possible."

"Okay, thank you. And, Bri, I have things to talk about with you, too."

Bri sighs. "Okay."

"So next Saturday at six at my place?"

"I'll be there."

CHAPTER FORTY-SEVEN

Bob Fisher and his sidekick, the tightly laced harridan, Ms. Miller, enter the central office conference room where I've been waiting. I sit up straight, his cryptic comments in the restaurant the previous evening having piqued my curiosity.

"Thank you for coming today," he says as they choose chairs across from me.

I smile at both of them. "No problem. How can I help?"

Fisher clears his throat, then looks at Ms. Miller, who raises her eyebrows and looks sour. "As I told you yesterday, we want to discuss the VR project."

"I'd be very happy to. I think it's going to be an immensely valuable tool."

Fisher's neck starts turning red as he says, "Not about the system, as we all agree VR will be useful. It's about, uh…about you and"—Ms. Miller bumps his arm—"about you and Ms. Walsh."

"What?"

Ms. Miller takes over. "A few community members have brought to our attention that you two are dating, and we are concerned that there is a conflict of interest on your part."

I feel my blood boil. "A conflict of interest?" *Stay calm, Renata.*

Fisher adds, "Well, you know, it could be construed that you're supporting Ms. Walsh's company because you have a relationship with her. There are other companies out there we could work with to purchase VR."

I stand and straighten my coat. "After more than thirty years of service to this school district, you're questioning my integrity?"

Fisher stands too. "Please, Renata."

I look to Ms. Miller, whose chin is tucked into her chest, then back to the board president. "Bob, there is no conflict of interest. We have involved the staff with evaluating VR, Darlene has compared JAWS products to other companies, we have a series of comparative quotes and we have spoken to universities who have contracted with JAWS. You have copies of everything yourself." I take a breath. "And those references strongly support the professionalism of the JAWS staff and speak highly of JAWS customer service. And they specifically point out Ms. Walsh's ethics and civic-mindedness in all their interactions with JAWS." I take another breath and finish with, "And by the way, I don't make the final decision. So don't approve the proposal if you believe JAWS is not the right match for this school district."

I walk to the door before turning again.

"But if you don't approve the proposal, then you will be responsible for impeding the opportunity for Westwood High School students to have best of VR technology to advance their educational experience." I look at Ms. Miller squarely and add, "I'm not sure you'll find a better company."

I walk out, fuming.

I am so angry. As I leave the building I feel like a volcano ready to erupt.

The car in front of me halts at the stop sign, and I brake abruptly, giving me time to take a breath. Maybe I should stop seeing Bri. I don't want to impede JAWS from getting the contract, and I don't want my stalker to find her.

CHAPTER FORTY-EIGHT

My mind goes through all the scenarios of how this evening could end as I stand looking out my bay window. Bri's blue Toyota Corolla catches my eye as she slows to turn into my driveway. I turn and quickly scan the dining table as I go to the patio door to meet Bri.

I open the door before Bri knocks. She stands and searches my eyes.

"I saw you coming down the street."

What is she thinking?

"Please come in."

I throw her coat over the La-Z-Boy chair as we walk through the living room.

"Dinner will be ready in about fifteen minutes," I say as I open the oven, my back to Bri. Then I turn, open the refrigerator, look inside, and ask, "Would you like something to drink?"

A hand lands on my shoulder. "Renata, we need to talk before we do anything."

When I turn, Bri and I stare at each other, her face flushed. I feel heat up my own neck.

"Please?"

I enter the dining room and point to a chair.

Bri sits up straight in the chair. I need to gather myself. I stand facing the window and take a deep breath.

Bri clears her throat. "We need to talk."

I pull up another chair to face Bri, our knees touching. "First, I want to apologize for interrupting you and your family the other Sunday. That was not my plan."

She looks straight into my eyes. "What *was* your plan?"

I return her stare. "I care about you, Bri, and I wanted to tell you. By the way, if I may ask, how are David and Liz?"

She leans back into the chair and says, "Everything is working out. He's attending AA and likes his new sponsor."

"I'm glad."

"So, I'm listening," she says.

I study my hands, which are folded on my lap. "Where do I start?" I take a deep breath. "My burnaversary is in two weeks."

Her face softens. "And?"

"I was babysitting Izzy. She was seven at the time. Ryan and Clare needed to go Christmas shopping. After we wrapped her gifts for her mom and dad, I put Izzy to bed and fell asleep on the couch."

Bri leans forward in her chair.

"I woke to a beeping sound. I realized it was the fire alarm. Smoke was everywhere, and all I could hear was crackling. I ran down the hall to Izzy's bedroom, and we ran into each other. We crawled toward the front door, but the fire and black smoke blocked our escape."

Suddenly I realize I've not shared my story with anyone outside my recovery team: my family, support group, therapist and of course, the fire department and police. But not my friends or work colleagues.

"We crawled to the second escape option—through Clare and Ryan's window. I opened the window and pushed Izzy out.

"I—as I lifted my leg to go through the window, I heard a splitting sound and felt a surge of heat." I stare at the ceiling, reliving that moment. "I looked up to the sounds coming from the ceiling, and all I saw was a ball of fire coming down on me."

Bri touches my arm.

"After that, all I remember is waking up in the hospital two weeks later. I had burns over thirty percent of my body."

She doesn't remove her hands. "I—I don't know what to say. I cannot imagine what you went through."

"The fire department stepped through the bedroom door as the fire and debris fell on top of me. They said I had curled into the fetal position with my left arm covering my face, and that protected the right side as they got the fire off me as quickly as they could."

Bri runs her hands up and down my arms. "When Izzy told Ash you were burned, I did some research. I didn't want to do anything or say anything that was not helpful or be insensitive or stupid."

The wall around my heart crumbles. "But…you're a licensed therapist. How could you say something wrong?"

She laughs. "Oh, being a therapist doesn't stop us from doing or saying insensitive things. We're human like everyone else."

"Then you've read about the skin grafts and scarring. And the psychological impact." I pause. "And the impact on relationships."

"Yeah, and on intimacy," Bri says.

Intimacy. My body yearns to touch Bri and for her to touch me. "I do want to be intimate with you." I press my forehead to hers and close my eyes. My hands fall to her hips. "You said you would go slow. You've researched what a person needs."

"Yes." Bri tilts my head up and kisses my forehead. "Thank you for sharing your story."

I step away from her. "There's something else. My partner at the time of the fire—Maggie. She…she had a hard time with… with me."

"What do you mean?"

I wince. "She had a hard time with the dual role of caregiver and lover. After I woke up she stopped coming to visit me in the hospital. She said she couldn't stand to see me in pain."

"And…"

I stare out the window. "I got home after another month or so in the hospital. When Maggie saw me naked for the first time"—I close my eyes and envision her standing in front of me, her eyes bulging and her mouth open, staring at me—"she said, 'I can't do this.' She ran out of the bedroom door and never came back."

"What? She did what?"

I turn, stand tall, and say, "She left and never came back. But we weren't getting along before the fire, so I think this"—I point to my body—"was the icing on the cake."

Bri wraps her arms around me. "I'm so sorry."

I let her hold me. Her embrace engulfs me in compassion and understanding—finally. The compassion and understanding I needed three years ago.

"No one has seen my body since."

Bri pulls me close.

I wrap my arms around her waist. "Please don't give up on me. On us."

She breaks our embrace and says, "Ren, I told you I've been thinking about you and me, and I don't want to give up on us. But when you accuse me of things that are just wrong and make erroneous assumptions, I feel attacked and manipulated. Sucker punched. I need you to trust me—to trust us. For us to continue, would you be willing to tell me when you're feeling anxious or overwhelmed about us?"

She's giving me a chance. My pulse quickens. I lock eyes with her and say, "Yes, I'm willing to do that." I hug her. "Can I ask you something?"

"Shoot."

"When you see me jumping to conclusions, will you tell me to stop, take a deep breath, and point it out to me?"

"Yes." She squeezes me and kisses my cheek. "I've missed you."

Thank you, support group, for showing me how to act like a survivor. To take control of my journey of redemption.

We hold each other for a few minutes, saying nothing, only holding and hearing each other's breathing and heartbeat.

Finally, Bri releases me and says, "You mentioned earlier that it will be your burnaversary. What can I do to support you?"

"During the Thanksgiving break, I reengaged with a peer support group run by the Phoenix Society for Burn Survivors."

She nods. "I read about them."

"They're helping me put my experiences and feelings into perspective. Back to your question about what you can do. Just…be with me? I don't know what I'll need. It could be a hug or a stern talking-to." I chuckle. "Or anything else in between. Just be within reach. Don't run and never come back."

Bri embraces me again. "I'm right here, and I'm not going anywhere." She hesitates, then gently touches the damaged left side of my neck. "Is this okay? Me touching your scar?"

I nod.

She leans in and kisses my top lip and then my bottom lip, and now her full lips are on mine. My legs weaken. My stomach flutters. I pull her closer to me.

When we separate, I step back and admit, "But we may need to cool it for a while, at least until the school board makes their decision about VR."

"What are you talking about?"

"Well, Bob Fisher and his homophobic sidekick accused me of having a conflict of interest because we're dating."

Bri's mouth hangs open. "You've got to be kidding."

"No," I say with a smirk. "I'm not."

"Well, I can meet with them and explain—"

I smile and pull her back into me. "No need. I informed them JAWS is the best company, and if they don't choose you, they will regret that decision."

"Thanks for standing up for me and the company."

I kiss her again, this time with a message of how much I miss her and want her.

We break our kiss, both of us panting.

I look to Bri's stomach. "Was that your stomach?"

"Yes, I'm hungry. I got caught up on a work project and haven't eaten since breakfast."

"Come on." I grab her hand. "Help me with the drinks."

As we enjoy our dinner Bri says, "Oh, by the way, David and Liz would like to have dinner with us."

"Really? After my intrusion?"

"Like David said, you make me happy." Bri kisses my cheek.

I tell myself, *I took another step.*

CHAPTER FORTY-NINE

After I told Darlene what Fisher and Ms. Miller said, I thought I would need to call 911. Her face reddened, she paced around her kitchen and threw a Tupperware bowl into the sink. I think her blood pressure went through the roof. Finally, after calming her down and giving her a shot of bourbon, she promised she'd behave.

Darlene and I make our final presentation to the board on Wednesday night. I had to force Darlene to promise me she would not go off script. She reiterates the utility, effectiveness, and usability of VR and its impact on student learning.

Then it's my turn. I stand and face the board, Mr. Fisher in the middle. "JAWS is the leading VR company in the area, and I know the president, Ms. Walsh, personally." I look directly at Mr. Fisher, then to Ms. Miller. "Ms. Walsh and her staff are experts in the VR arena and have the utmost integrity, as evidenced by the references we submitted to you. I strongly recommend JAWS as our partner in this endeavor as they demonstrate ingenuity, adaptability and flexibility to meet the needs of our students."

* * *

Thursday at the end of the day, I sit in Darlene's office. All is quiet except for a few students wandering the halls for after-school activities.

"The board votes on our proposal tonight?" Darlene asks.

"Yup."

"What do you think they'll do? Damn Mr. Fisher and Ms. Miller."

I sigh. "We've made numerous presentations and met with the treasurer regarding the budget. We've given them all the information they need to make a well-informed decision."

"Including the staff feedback," Darlene adds.

"Exactly. I trust they will do their due diligence and answer based on the merit of the impact on our student's educational advancement."

"Oh, that sounds *so* like an administrator," she says with a laugh.

I grin in spite of myself. "I know, right? But you saw Fisher and Miller during our presentation. They were pretty subdued."

"Yeah, especially after Barbara, the incoming board president, praised JAWS and Ms. Walsh's leadership. You know they don't want to piss off the next board president."

"I know. I'd say she's done her due diligence, wouldn't you?"

"Yeah." Darlene chuckles, then says, "You seem relaxed! You sure are smiling a lot."

"I'm feeling much better," I admit, "about myself."

"Does Bri have anything to do with that?"

"Yeah, she's being really understanding of my coming to terms with this." I point to the left side of my body. "My burnaversary is this week."

She looks surprised, maybe because I haven't really mentioned it until now. "Yeah? Is there anything I can do?"

"Bri and I are getting together. We haven't decided yet what we're going to do."

"I'm happy for you, Ren."

I think about how Darlene has been there for me. "I want to thank you again for all of your support during my recovery."

"Ren—"

"No. Let me finish. You came to the hospital to visit me. You took over some of my responsibilities at school. You brought food to the house when I got out of the hospital."

"That's what friends do for each other. You're stuck with me, kid."

"Thank you. You're a good friend." I squeeze her arm.

"When do you think the board will give us an answer?"

"I'm hoping they contact me by Friday."

"I'll keep my fingers crossed. Maybe if they approve it, we can celebrate. Could you invite Bri and her partners? If it gets approved, of course."

My phone rings. "Speaking of Bri," I murmur, unable to contain my grin.

Darlene waves her hand. "Go ahead."

"What's up?"

Her voice is husky. "I said we would be together this weekend, but I was wondering if we can change our plans?"

"You're changing our plans?" My heart skips a beat. She said she would be with me, that she would not leave.

"Ren. Deep breath. Don't jump to conclusions."

I exhale. "Okay. I'm trying not to."

"Our plan still includes us being together on your burnversary. I want to be with you."

"Okay. My heart is back to beating normally."

"Good. The new plan is adding people to our plan."

I hesitate. "Who are the people, and what is the new plan?"

"Jared, Sarah, Anthony, and I are going to dinner Saturday to celebrate our acquisition. With the Christmas holiday coming up, it's the only time Sarah can go."

"Only your partners?"

"Yes."

"Okay. I think more people would be okay."

"Great. I can pick you up Saturday around six?"

"Sounds like fun."

Bri says, "Ren. I can't wait to be with you."
I turn away from Darlene. "I can't wait to see you too. Bye."
"See ya Saturday."
I hold my phone to my chest.

CHAPTER FIFTY

Saturday morning, I get a call from Fisher, immediately after which I dial Darlene.

"Morning. What's up? Did anyone from the board contact you? I couldn't stop thinking about it all night last night."

"Yes, Bob Fisher called."

"And…"

"And…" I say teasingly, holding out a few seconds.

"Come on, Renata, you're killing me here."

I wait for a beat and say, "The VR project and budget are approved."

"You're kidding?"

"Nope. Unanimous."

"What? Fisher and Miller too?"

"I can only assume with Barbara's support. They didn't want to be the only two not in favor."

Silence. "Oh my God. You're not kidding!"

"Nope. Are you jumping up and down?"

"Yes! This is wonderful! Thank God."

"This is so exciting for the students."

"The science staff is gonna go bonkers when we tell them. We need to celebrate!" Darlene says.

"Well, that's the second reason I'm calling. I'm meeting with Bri and her partners tonight to celebrate their company's acquisition. I thought we could do a double celebration."

"Could we also celebrate your survival, since today is your burnaversary?"

I shake my head. "Nah, I don't think so. A burnaversary as a celebration? I need time to process that idea."

"Okay. What time and where for dinner?"

"Bri is picking me up at six, but I don't know where. I'll call her and text you the location." I close my eyes tight with anticipation. "Darlene, thanks for all your work on this project. See you later."

* * *

I call Bri, and she picks up on the second ring.

"Good morning, beautiful," Bri says, causing my heart to stop a beat. She thinks I'm beautiful, and I'm starting to believe I am.

"Morning. Hey, can I invite Darlene to the celebration dinner? We have a secret."

"Sure. A secret? You can't give me a hint?" she asks playfully.

"No. I cannot."

"Can I bribe you with the promise of a wonderful night full of laughter and outstanding food?"

"I'm expecting that already."

"Okay. How about a wild pair of socks?"

What I want is for her to stay the night. I don't want to be alone tonight. Can I ask her to stay?

"I would expect nothing less with the socks."

I can do this. Be brave.

Silence.

"You there?"

I swallow hard. "Um…can you stay the night?"

More silence. Then, "Did I hear you correctly? You want me to stay the night with you?"

"Yes."

"Are you sure?"

"I'm not sure what that means, except I don't want to be alone tonight."

"If it means a sleepover, I'm in."

"Really?"

"Sure. Is this related to today being your burnaversary?"

"Maybe. I'm not sure. Probably."

"What's going on in your head right now?"

"I'm excited about celebrating with you and your friends instead of being with Clare and her family."

"What do you mean?"

"I usually spend the day with Clare and her family," I explain. "But that's hard as all of us are somehow involved in the fire— Izzy with me, trying to escape, and then Ryan and Clare losing their house and almost everything they owned." I take a deep breath.

"You don't need to talk about it if you don't want to."

"No. I need to tell you. They all felt guilty about my almost dying."

"I can appreciate that, but at least on the surface, you all seem reasonably fine now."

"We still have our days. But we did go to therapy, both individually and as a family. They've been totally supportive and I don't know what I would have done without them."

"But?"

"My group members suggested that I consider changing what I do on that day."

They also said to celebrate my survival. One step at a time.

Bri's voice is sincere. "I imagine this can be a difficult day for you, Ren. Please. I will do whatever you need me to do."

"Okay."

"Do you still want me to stay the night?"

I take a deep breath and answer unhesitatingly, "Yes."

"Good, because I want to spend more time with you. I'll bring an overnight bag. I do sleep nude, but I'll bring something to wear."

"Oh, um, interesting." I've seen her strong legs and firm ass. What does the rest of her look like?

She laughs. "Ren, no expectations. Only spending time together."

"I'd like that. Oh, where are we having dinner, so I can tell Darlene where to meet us?"

"Meadowlark on Far Hills in Dayton. I'll text you the address."

"Thank you. I can't wait to see you."

CHAPTER FIFTY-ONE

I glance at Bri as she drives. Her long fingers on the steering wheel bring back the memory of her fingers massaging my breast.

"Bri, can I ask more about your relationship with Olivia?"

"Sure. What do you want to know?"

"If I remember correctly, you said you were together for about ten years, right?"

"Yeah, you remember correctly."

"You needed to decide on investing in your company, which meant investing your joint money or was it your personal money?"

"I was hoping she would help support me financially while things got going, and she was not interested in investing her money in the company. And that's when Olivia gave me an ultimatum—the company or her."

"Really?"

"Yeah. She was not a risk-taker, which I knew when we got together."

"She didn't believe you'd be successful?" I rub my arm. My scars start to itch. Damn it, I was so nervous about tonight, I forgot to put on lotion.

"I don't think she wanted to wait to find out. She wanted things. She always wanted more. I couldn't give her that on my university salary."

"And she had issues with your brother?"

"Yeah, she didn't like the roller-coaster ride of dealing with him and his alcoholism."

But if you love someone, you stay on the ride. Just like Bri is staying on mine.

"I thought she was a nurse?"

"Still is."

"You'd think she'd understand David's issues."

Bri laughs with only a tinge of bitterness. "She always said that wasn't her specialty."

It sounds to me like Olivia was looking for a way out of the relationship, but I don't say that. Instead, I ask, "So, where is she now? You said she came into town. From where?"

"She's living in Colorado and working as an ER nurse. And dating a lawyer."

"I'm assuming a woman?"

"Yes."

"Sounds like she's moved on with her life."

Bri nods. "Yeah, and according to her, she has all the material things she wanted and more, so she's happy."

"What about you?"

"Me? What do you mean?"

"Do you have all the things you want? Are you happy?"

Bri reaches over and squeezes my leg. "Investing in the company was the right decision for my partners and me. I was financially strapped for about six years, but now I'm reaping the rewards."

She pulls into the Meadowlark parking lot and finds a spot next to a lamppost. We stand under the light. "But are you happy?" I ask her gently.

She grabs my hand and we begin to walk. "The money takes away the worry for my future, financially speaking, and it allows me to give back so others can be successful."

"Is there a *but*?"

"But—I miss having someone in my life to come home to, to share my life with." Bri stops and touches my cheek. "Being with you makes me happy."

"Darlene is at the door," I finally say, pointing to the entrance.

* * *

As we all eat, Jared asks, "So what is everyone doing for the Christmas holidays?"

Sarah looks up from her steak and says, "My kids are making their lists as we speak. And the lists keep getting longer and longer."

Jared and Anthony both say they'll be spending time with families—Jared in Kentucky and Anthony in Chicago.

Darlene says, "I'm going to visit my parents in Florida."

"That'll be fun, you always like spending time with your parents," I say. "Plus you get out of this cold!"

She beams excitedly. "Exactly."

I turn to her and whisper so no one else can hear me, "And spending time with Shelly."

Darlene blushes. "Of course."

I put my hand on Bri's thigh and ask, "What are you doing for Christmas?"

"Um…I usually stop by Sarah's, give the kids presents, and have a bite to eat. Then I go home."

Before I think about it, I blurt, "Would you like to spend it with me?"

There's a pause, and then Bri says, "I was assuming you would go to Clare's."

"Yes, but I'm sure they wouldn't mind you joining us."

Bri hesitates. A smile grows on her face. "I can drop off the kids' gifts and then go with you to Clare's." She looks at Sarah. "You don't mind?"

"No way." Sarah winks at her. "Go eat with Ren's family."

Bri turns back to me. "Thanks, I would like that."

"I would too." I squeeze her thigh.

She grabs her drink and asks, "Everyone has a drink? This is a night to celebrate JAWS moving to the next level."

"Hear, hear," Jared says loudly.

Bri looks each of her partners in the eye as she says, "I am so honored to be your partner. You all put in so much time and effort to reach this point. Thank you for taking the risk."

"We couldn't have done it without you," Sarah says.

Bri raises her drink. We all do the same. "To us and the bright future ahead," she toasts.

After everyone has taken a drink, I say, "Well, Darlene and I want to share some exciting news as well. Darlene, you want to do the honors?"

"Sure." She clears her throat. "Drumroll, please."

Bri looks at me inquisitively. Jared and Sarah tap the top of the table with their hands.

"The school board approved our proposal to use VR in the science department, starting next year! Renata received the phone call this morning."

They all hoot, holler, and clap. Bri wraps her arm around my shoulder, pulls me close, and kisses my cheek.

All eyes at our table are on us.

Bri and I look at each other. Finally, Bri's face turns red.

Sarah points her finger to Bri and me, her eyebrows raised, and asks, "You two?"

The others wait, anticipation in their eyes.

"Yes, us two," I answer.

They all clap again. Anthony and Jared high-five each other.

"About time!" Sarah exclaims.

"Yes, about time," Darlene says with a smile, and a tear in her eye.

CHAPTER FIFTY-TWO

Bri pulls into my driveway, turns to me and asks, "You still want me to stay?" Her eyes are hopeful.

I touch her arm and nod. "Yes, I want you to stay."

Bri touches my cheek and says, "Okay." She turns off the car, reaches into the back seat, grabs her overnight bag, and follows me to the front door.

"I had a good time tonight," I say, holding the door open for her and resisting the urge to rub my now ferociously itchy scars.

As Bri passes me, she says, "Me too. Having us all together was fun—it reminded me of a family celebration."

I hang up our coats and go to the kitchen, where Bri stands with her overnight bag at her feet. "Would you like something to drink?" I point to the living room. "Or do you want to sit down and watch some TV?" I move between the refrigerator and pantry. "Actually, do you want anything to eat?"

Bri reaches for me. "Renata. Stop."

"Stop what?" I ask, rubbing my neck.

"Stop pacing and asking me questions."

I stop in the middle of the kitchen and take a deep breath. Bri grabs my hand and leads me to the couch. "You've been rubbing your arm all night and now your neck. What is happening with you?"

"I'm attracted to you."

"And I'm attracted to you," Bri responds.

"I like you...a lot, probably more than a lot, and"—my eyes lock onto Bri's like a magnet—"I want you to touch me."

"But?"

I lower my eyes to my hands, which I can't seem to stop moving. "But no one's touched me since...I'm the only one who touches my scars. I'm clueless about how it feels when someone else does."

"So, you're nervous? Is that why you're rubbing your arm and neck?"

"No. The scars itch," I admit. "I forgot to put lotion on them before we went to dinner."

"Okay, I have a suggestion. We can start with lotion. Why don't you let me put the lotion on your scars?"

"Uh—"

"On your shoulder? See how it feels to you."

"Okay, yeah." I stand and take Bri's hand. "I can do that."

I lead her to the bedroom, where I turn on the lamp on the nightstand next to my bed. We stand facing each other, and Bri asks, "How do you want to do this?"

My heart pounds against my chest. "Um...I'm not sure."

"Lotion?" She looks around the bedroom. "Where's the lotion?"

"Yeah, lotion." I go into the en suite, return, and hand Bri the lotion.

Searching my eyes, she asks, "Would you be comfortable taking off your sweater and bra and keeping your back to me?"

I turn, my hands shaking as I slowly lift my sweater over my head and place it on the bed. I unbutton my blouse, and Bri holds it at the collar as I remove my arms from the sleeves. She hands me the blouse, and I cover the front of my body. Now the scars covering the left side of my back are visible. I gaze over my shoulder and ask, "Can you unhook my bra, please?"

Bri does so, barely touching me.

I pull my right arm out of my bra while holding my blouse with my left hand, then I do the same with my left arm while my right arm covers my breasts.

I hear a squirt of lotion, and Bri says, "I'll warm up the lotion." She rubs her hands together. "Ready?"

"Uh…ready as I'll ever be."

"Ren." Bri steps forward on my right side. "Let's talk our way through this together."

"I'll do my best." I bite my lower lip and hold my breath.

Bri steps back, and I release my breath as she touches my neck with her fingers. I pull up my shoulder at her touch.

"Relax, Ren."

I lower my shoulders and exhale again.

She uses her full hand and moves over my shoulder, rubbing the lotion in circles over the scars, then proceeds to my back and down my left side. "What are you feeling?" She adds more lotion on her hands and moves down the back of my arm.

"I sense your fingers and hands making circles. But the sensation—"

"So, you recognize my touch, but it doesn't all feel the same?"

"Right. And in some places, there's no sensation."

"Is that usual?" Bri asks as she applies lotion to my upper back.

"Well, the third-degree burns damaged the nerve endings. The doctor said it would take a while for them to come back, and some may never."

Her touch is so gentle.

Bri moves to my side and says, "Why don't we sit on the bed so I can put lotion on all of your arm?"

Bri lowers herself beside me. I rest my scarred arm on her lap, hand down. Her soft eyes never leave mine. I'm afraid to blink. I don't want to lose this connection.

Bri adds more lotion to her hands, then starts at the top of my hand before roaming over the top of my arm to my shoulder. She adds more lotion and reverses her path, starting at my shoulder and back down to my hand. I watch her long fingers caress my arm. It's soothing and stirs a need for more.

"How does it feel?" she asks as she continues to massage my arm.

"The lotion and your touch feel amazing. And my skin is saying thank you. I can't reach all of my back. How do the scars feel to you?"

"Some are soft, and others are hard. Some are flat, and others stick out more," she says as touches the scar on my ribs. "Some are smooth, and some are rough."

"That's my perception too."

"Do you want me to lotion any other part of you? Your hip? Your stomach?" She stops rubbing. "Or do you want to apply it yourself?"

God, yes. I want you to touch every part of my body.

I gaze up into her eyes. "You've seen the scars on my neck, back, arm, and side."

"Yes. I have."

"You said we should talk, right?"

"Right."

"Okay, so here goes—I'm not sure I can have you touch those parts without wanting—I mean, I sense your caring when you put lotion on me, but—"

She turns me to face her and holds my damaged hand. "Take your time."

"You touch my hand like you touched my back and arm. The scars don't repulse or scare you?"

"No. You don't repulse or scare me, so why should your scars?"

"The scars not scaring you confuses me," I say with a sheepish laugh, leaning into her and resting my head on her shoulder.

There's a pause. "Renata, what do you want to happen right now? What do you need?"

I drop my other hand. My blouse falls between us. I take her hand holding mine and place it on my disfigured breast.

Bri swallows hard. "Are you sure about this?"

"Yes, I am. I need you to touch me, Brianna Walsh." I lean closer, tangle my hands in her hair, and kiss her.

Bri's hand surrounds my breast and gently squeezes. "How does that feel? Does it hurt?" she whispers against my lips.

"No. Don't stop." I kiss Bri again, extending my tongue, searching for an entrance. She opens her mouth and our tongues touch. She pulls me closer with her other arm. My groin is aching with each kiss. I want—no, I *need*—this woman.

We break our kiss. Bri's eyes are intense. She kisses my cheek and moves down to my neck, my shoulder…light kisses trace the scars down to my breast.

"May I?"

I nod.

"Tell me if it hurts or is uncomfortable."

I nod again.

Bri extends her tongue and licks my nipple. "Do you sense my tongue?"

"Not really."

"How about this?"

"Oh—yeah. I felt your teeth." My nipple comes to attention.

Bri lifts her head, smiles, and says, "This one needs a different approach," and returns to lick and nibble my scarred breast. She circles it with kisses, sucking and biting my nipple in between her circling.

I arch into her mouth. "Bri, yes," I gasp. "Your teeth." I hold her head in place as her other hand caresses my other breast. Unable to stand it, I pull Bri up by her hair. "I need you naked and in bed."

Bri stands, pulls off her sweater, and unhooks her bra. When she starts to unzip her pants, I jump up and grab her hands. "Let me." I lower her pants and then her underwear, which is soaking wet and smells delicious. I laugh when I take off her socks that say, *Make Love, Not War.*

Bri looks hurt. "Why are you laughing?"

"Oh, honey—your socks."

She throws her head back and laughs. I shove back the bed covers and hurriedly remove the rest of my clothes. Finally, I crawl in bed and open my arms. "Come here."

Bri climbs onto the bed and crawls on all fours until we lie face-to-face. Her hand moves up and down, caressing my hip and my ass, nothing stopping her.

"I feel your touch," I murmur, grabbing her ass and pulling her close so our bodies touch, chest to our toes. "Please don't stop." Our hands roam each other's bodies uncontrollably as we share hot, wet kisses.

"I never thought anyone would want to touch me," I moan, "or that I would want anyone to touch me again."

"Ren," Bri says as she caresses my face, "you are beautiful." Her hand captures my breast and she moves her leg between mine.

I roll over and pull Bri on top of me. Her juices cover my leg. Her weight on me feels like I've come home. "You're awakening nerves I didn't know I would ever feel again," I murmur as my body sizzles.

Bri positions herself between my legs, her hips moving into me. Between kisses, she whispers, "How do you like to be touched?"

I grab her hand and suck her index finger into my mouth. "Fingers." I brush my thumb over her swollen lips and mumble, "Mouth." Then I scrape my fingernails down her back and say, "Hands, tongue, and all ways possible." Her intense gaze sparks an inner fire I never want to be smothered. I open my legs wider.

"I want—I *need* to touch you. I need to be inside you," Bri moans between ragged breaths. She kisses me, her tongue exploring my mouth. I wrap my arms tightly around her and suck her tongue, urging her to continue.

She breaks the kiss and licks her way between my breasts, stopping to kiss each of them, sending a bolt of lightning to my clit.

"Please—"

Her next move is kissing, licking, and sucking my pubic area, driving me close to the edge.

"Yes," I gasp, "inside, I need you inside me."

Bri enters me with one finger, still kissing my traumatized pubic skin.

I wrap my hand in the bedsheets and moan, "Oh, God, Bri." I raise myself onto my elbows and, over my mound, meet her eyes twinkling as she starts to lick my swollen clit.

She adds another finger.

I fall back onto the bed, my hips rise with each lick. Bri's fingers dance with the cadence of her tongue.

The build-up starts in my stomach, moving to the walls of my vagina, pulsating around Bri's fingers. The tension builds in my arms and legs, my whole body trembling.

She continues to lick and suck and penetrate.

I lean up and dig my fingers into her hair, holding her in place. My legs shake. My belly tightens. I slam back onto the bed, arching my hips and closing my eyes, and my body explodes.

The next thing I know, I'm holding Bri in my arms. Her head rests on my chest.

As she traces the scars, she murmurs, "Are you okay?"

"I am wonderful."

"You are so damn sexy, how you and your body react to my touch."

As she lies in my arms, I realize my chest is wet. I take a deep breath and pull her close to kiss the top of her head. "Are *you* okay?"

She lifts her head, and our eyes meet. "You are a warrior. Your scars tell me how you fought to survive. I am in awe of your courage and determination."

I sigh and wipe her tears. "Your belief in me has restored my courage and determination. I can't thank you enough for touching me."

"Oh, my pleasure. I've wanted to touch you since the first time we met."

I gaze into her eyes, intertwining her fingers with mine. "I've never experienced such a connection with anyone as I felt tonight with you."

Bri climbs on top of me and, after a long and fervent kiss, says, "Well, my socks did say to make love, not war."

CHAPTER FIFTY-THREE

A warm body engulfs me from behind. "Good morning, gorgeous," Bri whispers in my ear.

I snuggle into her. "Morning." We lie like that for a few minutes, her arm around my waist and her hand on my stomach, and I say, "Last night and early this morning, was...was—"

"Everything I imagined and more," she says. I find her hand on my stomach and squeeze it. "How was it for you?"

"I was nervous at first—I didn't know what to expect when you touched the scars." Bri strokes my shoulder and kisses my neck. "I asked myself many times if it would be the same. Or would it be different? Be painful?"

Bri crawls on top of me, facing me. There's a broad grin on her face when she asks, "And?"

"And what?"

She wiggles a leg between mine. "And what did you find out after us?"

I grin back at her. "After us what?"

"After last night and this morning," she says, her voice smoky and her eyes radiant.

"Well, I found out your mouth"—I kiss her, then grab her hand and place it on my scarred breast—"and your hand demonstrates your thoughtfulness and gentleness."

"Did you feel pain when we touched or when there was friction?"

"Friction? You mean our sweaty bodies rubbing together?" I run the back of my hand over her cheek. "Nothing would make me want to stop you from making love with me."

She dips her head, and her face flushes. "I-I—you will tell me if I do anything that hurts, right?"

"Yes. I will tell you."

She strokes my hair and places a soft kiss on my forehead. "I'm looking forward to more experimenting."

"How about breakfast?"

"Sure."

I slither out of bed and walk to the bathroom. "I need a shower."

Bri jumps out of bed, her hips swaying. "Anytime you need lotion on your sexy body, pick me."

"Oh, I pick you," I said, pointing my index finger at her. Bri opens her mouth and encloses my finger with her lips, twirling her tongue around it. My body heats up. "Want to join me?"

"Absolutely."

CHAPTER FIFTY-FOUR

"You make the best waffles," Bri says as she takes another bite of her strawberry- and chocolate-covered waffle with whipped cream. Bowls, spoons, and baking ingredients line the counter. "But I thought I was the only one to make a mess of a kitchen." A dollop of whipped cream hangs on her top lip as she grins and raises her eyebrows. "But the result is what counts, and the result is delicious. Like you." She runs her tongue over her top lip, licking off the whipped cream. I blush, my stomach tightening.

She swivels her chair and rotates mine so we are face-to-face. "I'm enjoying our time together. Last night—wow!" She leans in, and her lips lock on mine.

I entwine our fingers and take in her generous lips until I break our kiss. "Wow! I like that."

Her hand slides under my shirt and touches my side. "Me too."

I wince.

"What's wrong?"

"Sorry, my grafts are a little tender this morning." I place a soft kiss on her lips.

Bri pulls back with a look of concern. "Is that normal?"

"Yeah, from what I read and from talking with other women in the support group, the skin grafts can be sore."

"Okay, so we take a break," she says, grinning.

I touch her arm. "I'm sorry."

"Don't apologize. We need to listen to your body, and besides, there are other ways to be intimate."

"Like what?"

"Let's see. Um…We can make out and enjoy the thrill of kissing without expecting more."

I smile. "Not sure I can stop myself from expecting more."

"Okay, next. We can cook together." Bri counts off on her fingers. "Dance. Talk about what's important to each of us. Or cuddle."

"Cuddling while you feed me M&M's?"

"Yes," she laughs. "It doesn't matter to me, as long as we're together."

"You mean that?"

"Yes, Ren. I want to be with you, doing whatever or doing nothing."

I hug Bri and say, "Let's finish our breakfast before it gets cold."

We chat over the next step for me to apply for a grant from her company. "Next week, can you email me a copy of the grant application?"

"I almost forgot!" She shakes her head. "I can't focus on anything else when I'm with you. I want to be with you all the time. But I'm going to be out of the office next week. But, back to your question. The application is on the foundation website."

I kiss her, then ask, "Where will you be? You mean I can't see you until when?"

"Oh, you gonna miss me, are you?" Bri smiles.

I bolt off my chair and take my dishes to the sink. "I might." My body tenses with each step.

Bri collects her dishes and comes to the sink too. "Did I say something wrong?"

"No." I take a deep breath, step away from the sink, and walk into the living room.

Bri follows and sits next to me on the couch, grabbing my hands and rubbing her thumbs over them. "Renata. Talk to me. What's happening?"

I look directly at her. "You see me." I point to myself. "You see the scars. They don't stop you from seeing me."

"And that scares you?"

"I don't know if it scares me. I didn't think it would happen— someone wanting me. Someone looking through the scars and into *me*."

Bri moves and kneels in front of me, her hands on my thighs. "Renata, it *can* happen. It is happening."

"I'm starting to believe it's happening." I laugh. I surround Bri's face with my hands and place a gentle kiss on her lips and her cheek. "So, where will you be next week?"

"Sarah and I are presenting to two high schools and two universities in Pennsylvania," she says, lowering her gaze.

"What's wrong? You look worried about something."

"I'm not sure I should go because of the stalker."

I shake my head. "I've not had any phone calls or unwanted gifts recently. And you haven't either. Don't worry. I'll be fine. Sergeant Jackson is on speed dial. I'll be fine. I have Clare, Ryan, and Darlene all ready to be by my side if anything happens."

Bri stands, pulls me up, and envelops me in her arms. My body relaxes, and I embrace her warmth.

"Are you sure?"

"Yes, I'm sure." Bri exhales, and I lean back in her arms and ask, "So, when will you be back?"

"We fly out Monday and return late Saturday night."

"Do you need someone to take and pick you up at the airport?"

"No. I'm leaving my car at the airport."

"Are you sure?"

"Yeah." Bri kisses me. "But thanks for offering."

"Why don't you join me at Clare's for Sunday dinner?"

"Are you sure? That would be great. Speaking of Sunday dinner, what about today? Is Clare expecting you today?"

"No, I told Clare I wouldn't be there today."

"Okay. So, what do you want to do the rest of the day?" Bri asks.

"Let's cuddle and watch a football game."

"Cuddling on the couch?"

"Yeah, I can handle that."

I rush to the counter, gather the breakfast dishes, and throw them into the dishwasher, yelling, "Cuddle time in five minutes."

Bri yells back, "And don't forget the M&M's!"

CHAPTER FIFTY-FIVE

Early Monday morning I'm drinking my coffee before heading to school when the doorbell rings. My mind immediately goes to the stalker. I take a deep breath as I walk through the dining room to the window.

I see Bri's car. She's holding something in her hand.

I hustle and open the door. "Come in." I kiss her as she comes in. "What are you doing here? Aren't you off to Pennsylvania this morning?"

"Yes, but I bought something for you and wanted to give it to you before I left." She hands me a long, slim rectangular box. "When you use it I hope it reminds you of me." When she smiles, her eyes light up.

My imagination goes crazy. What could this be? Something that would remind me of her. I feel my face start to heat up.

"You're blushing. What are you thinking?"

I giggle. "Nothing."

"Oh…" Bri laughs with me as she glances at her watch. "Just open it, I gotta go."

I'm not sure what I'm seeing. "It looks like a small paint roller."

"No." She chuckles. "It's not for paint. Take it out. It's to put lotion on your back." She takes the roller and points to the soft roller. "See, you put the lotion on the roller"—she pretends she's squeezing a bottle—"then you reach back"—she demonstrates—"and you roll on the lotion." Bri smiles broadly. "So when you need to put lotion on your back and on one's here, you can."

"Bri, that...that is so thoughtful." I wrap my arm around her. "Thank you."

She leans back and kisses me lightly, and the anticipation of what's next excites me, but I push her away. "You gotta go or you'll miss your flight."

She kisses me again. "Right." She turns and opens the door but stops and walks back to me. "I lo—I...I'm going to miss you."

Was she going to say love?

I hug her and whisper in her ear, "I'm going to miss you too."

We break our embrace. "Okay, I need to go," she says and hustles out the door.

When the door closes, I move to the window to watch her pull away. "I love you too."

CHAPTER FIFTY-SIX

"This week is going fast," Darlene says as we stand in the gym, watching a girls' basketball game.

Not fast enough for me. I can't wait to be with Bri.

A player intercepts the opponent's pass, and the gym erupts with a loud cheer. "Good defense!" I yell, clapping.

"Are you staying for the whole game?" she asks.

"Until halftime, then I'm off. I want to start on the VR grant application today. But too many other things to deal with, so I'm taking it home."

"You want some help?"

"Not tonight. How about tomorrow after school, you could come over and we can work on it together?"

* * *

I sit on the couch with my feet curled underneath me, contemplating how to answer one of the grant application questions.

On Monday, Bri had texted me that she'd arrived in Harrisburg, but I haven't heard anything since. Distracted, I walk to the front window. Gentle snow begins to fall. I wrap my arms around myself.

I didn't ask her to make contact with me every night, although I hoped she would want to after our weekend together. I think of her hands caressing my body with lotion and my body shaking with pleasure. And those socks—and Bri on top of me, making love to me. The snowfall increases, and the streetlight makes it sparkle like tiny stars in the night.

My phone vibrates in my back pocket. Bri.

"Hi."

"Hi, Ren. I hope it's not too late to call you."

"No." I turn and walk back into the living room. "I'm working on the grant application."

"Oh. Do you have any questions?"

"Not yet. I just got started."

"I'm sorry I didn't text or call yesterday. It was so hectic. First, our rental car got a flat tire. Then there was an accident that had traffic at a standstill for two hours."

"Wow. Frustrating." I walk to the living room and collapse onto the recliner.

"Yeah. And by the time we got to the hotel, it was too late. And today we were booked solid with appointments and more car rides." Bri takes a deep breath. "How are you?"

"I'm fine."

"I wanted to ask you before I forget—is Clare okay with me joining you for Christmas?"

"Yes! She is delighted and, of course, Izzy is super excited."

Bri laughs. "I'm looking forward to it. I better do some shopping when I return."

"Oh, that isn't necessary."

"Of course it is. It's Christmas."

"Bri—"

"I'm changing the subject. Is it snowing?"

"Yeah, but it's not supposed to accumulate much."

"I hope not. I'm anxious to come home."

"You are?"

"Yes. I miss you," she says softly.

"You miss me?" My face lights up with a giant smile. "And here I thought I would be the one missing you."

"Oh, so you don't miss me?" Bri's voice turns serious.

Do I tell her I'm falling in love with her?

"Bri. I miss you too."

"Whew. I was getting a little nervous."

"Oh, and thank you for the lotion roller or whatever it's called. It's not the same as your hands, but my back appreciates it."

"Good, I'll be home soon and then I can take over."

"To be honest, I can't wait to tackle you and kiss you all over," I say, imagining myself throwing her on my bed, ripping off her clothes, and running my tongue up her stomach from the V between her thighs, over her breasts, and up her long neck until I capture her mouth with mine.

"Did you hear what I said?"

"Sorry, my mind is—um, anyway, what did you say?"

"I said, I like hearing that you can't wait to see me because I feel the same. Look, I have to go. Sarah and I need to review some new information for our presentation to East Stroudsburg University tomorrow morning. By the way, have you had any contact from your stalker?"

Do I tell her about my dream the other night? The one where I'm lying in the hospital bed, my mind muddy from the medication, and a voice keeps telling me to wake up? And then suddenly I wake up, and I'm in my own bed?

"No, I haven't."

"Good. But promise me if you get something, you'll contact Sergeant Jackson and call me."

"I will. Good luck tomorrow, Bri."

CHAPTER FIFTY-SEVEN

"So, how was the rest of your week after your call with Bri?" Clare asks me on the phone as I search my pantry for chicken noodle soup.

"Um…Darlene came over Thursday after school, and we worked on the VR grant application."

"And Bri?"

"She texted or called each night."

"What is that clanging?"

I'm on my knees, my phone between my ear and shoulder, as I ransack my cabinet. "Oh, I can't find my small pot to make my dinner."

"Oh. Back to you and Bri. What did you two talk about?"

"Anything and everything, I guess."

"Sis, I am so happy for you."

I find the pot and put it on the stove. "I *am* happy. Still a little nervous, but Darlene says my sparkle is back in my eyes."

"She's right. You're more relaxed and—I don't know, you're more comfortable with yourself."

"But—" I find the can opener to dump the soup into the pot.

"But what?"

My mind drifts back to yesterday.

I went to retrieve my mail, and when I opened the mailbox, I saw a box of Esther Price candy. My mind raced to the stalker. My breathing increased and my jaws clenched, my anger rising. Finally, I slammed the mailbox lid closed, called Sergeant Jackson, and waited for her to arrive.

As I waited, I paced on the sidewalk, and an internal battle started about whether to interrupt Bri's business trip or not. She asked me to contact her if anything happened. But I had called the police, so did I need to tell Bri?

I needed to tell her because I promised her I would. I wanted to build our relationship on a solid foundation of trust and truth.

My call went to her voice mail, and I left a message saying I got candy from the stalker but that I called the police and that I'm fine.

"I got another gift from my secret admirer," I admit to Clare. "This time it was candy."

"Oh, Ren. This is getting out of hand."

I run my hand through my hair. "I agree. I called the police and she came over and took the box of candy and the card."

"What is she going to do?"

"She'll go to the store to get any information. But unless the person is using a credit card…"

"Right. Do you feel safe? You want to come and stay with us?"

"No, I'm okay."

"When does Bri get in?"

"Late tonight. She texted around five thirty this evening and said her flight was delayed due to some mechanical problem with the plane. It'll be late."

"You guys will be here tomorrow for Sunday dinner, right?"

"Yup. Bri will text me Sunday morning."

"Okay. We're all looking forward to it."

* * *

My phone rings as I watch the eleven o'clock news in my sweatpants and a heavy zipped hoodie. I jerk to attention. I check the ID—Bri.

Bri says before I can say a word, "Hey just checking in to see how you're doing. Any more surprise gifts or calls? No more Esther Price candy?"

"No."

"How are you?"

"Bri, I'm fine."

"Are you sure?"

"I'm sure. Is your flight still scheduled to leave?"

"Yes, probably in about half an hour. I'll get in pretty late, so I'll see you tomorrow."

"Okay, text me when you get home. No matter what time."

"Will do."

I return my phone to my hoodie pocket and walk to the front window. The snow is still falling.

I think about Bri and how I've missed spending time with her. My hand goes down my arm and over my breast and down to my hip. I close the curtains and go into the bathroom, where I stand in front of the mirror, take off my hoodie and stand taller. "These are my scars," I say out loud, pounding my palm on my chest. "My scars—from *my* battle to survive." I move my open hand to my stomach and move up to my shoulder. "Mine."

I step back and take a deep breath. I thought my scars represented the love I lost, but now I realize Maggie never loved me. She never saw me.

I put my hoodie back on.

The fire did not change my heart.

I go back to the window and throw open the curtains. The snow dances in the light. I imagine Bri and me hugging tomorrow. Bri, who sees me and sees through my scars, has touched my heart.

Warmth runs through my body. I smile and say out loud to no one but myself, "I'm a survivor. I realize now that my scars have led me to the love I deserve. My journey of redemption leads me back to me and…to you."

CHAPTER FIFTY-EIGHT

I roll onto my back, stretch, and gaze at the clock. It's almost ten a.m. I haven't slept this well since—oh, yeah, I was in Bri's arms.

Bri. I check my phone lying on the nightstand. No texts or messages. My heart skips a beat. She must have gotten in late and is still sleeping.

I throw off the covers and shower, smiling, anticipating seeing her. I glance out the front window to see four inches of pristine snow on the ground. I continue to the kitchen for breakfast.

My mind goes to Bri again. I fantasize about different kiss scenarios and saying the words, "I love you," when my phone rings and brings me back to reality.

"Hey, sis. Would you stop by the store and pick up some ice cream on your way over?"

"Sure. Let me guess?"

I hear Izzy yell, "Chocolate!"

"You heard her?"

I laugh. "Yes."

"Did you hear from Bri? It snowed last night and got below freezing."

"I haven't."

"Are you concerned?"

"No." I shake my head. "I think she got in late—her flight was delayed. She's probably sleeping in."

"Okay. Thanks for picking up the ice cream. See you later."

* * *

I call Bri around noon and get no answer. I leave a message asking her to call me back as soon as possible. I busy myself cleaning the house, shoveling the driveway, and not jumping to conclusions. Bri cares for me and—hopefully—loves me as I love her.

After I text her two hours later to no answer, I start to worry.

I glance at my watch. Three thirty.

Something is wrong. My chest is tight.

I head to Clare's and burst through the front door. Clare is in the kitchen working on dinner, and Ryan is watching a football game with Izzy. Clare drops a pot onto the stove with a clatter. "Ren! What's wrong?"

Ryan and Izzy whirl around as I sprint through the family room to the kitchen. "I called and texted Bri, and she is not answering me. I'm worried."

"Let's not jump to conclusions," Ryan says.

"I know. I'm trying not to."

"Did Bri go on her business trip with anyone else?" he asks.

My brain clears for a moment. "Yeah—yeah, Sarah."

"Did you call her?" Clare asks.

"No. I didn't think about that."

"Do you have her number?" Ryan asks patiently.

"Uh—I—I think I do because she was the lead on our VR project. Let me check my phone." I hit contacts and search. My fingers and eyes do not move as fast as I want them to. "Yes, here it is. I'll call her."

As I push the button to call Sarah, my phone rings. Bri's name appears on the screen. "Bri?" I listen to a voice that isn't hers. "Oh, Sarah—I was just dialing your number. I've been trying to get ahold of Bri because she's not answering my calls or texts. I'm worried."

I listen.

"What? When?" I grab Ryan's arm, my heart pounding. "Okay—okay. I'm on my way." I turn to Clare and Ryan, frantic. "I'm going to the hospital. It's Bri."

As I put my car in drive, Sarah's words play in my head. Black ice. Accident. Room 323.

Room 323.

Room 323.

I slam the gas pedal to the floor.

CHAPTER FIFTY-NINE

I jog down the hall to room 323, then stop at the door and take a deep breath before I knock. There is Bri, sleeping.

Tears come to my eyes.

She's lying in bed. Her arms are bruised, her lip swollen, and she is black and blue around her eyes. A dark red mark starts at her neck and disappears under her hospital gown. A monitor to the right of the bed shows her blood pressure, oxygen level, and heartbeat.

Sarah comes to me and wraps her arm around my shoulder. "It looks worse than it is," she says as she wipes away a tear.

"How is she?"

"She returned a few minutes ago from a CT scan of her knee—it hit the dashboard."

"Anything else?"

"They were concerned about whiplash and a concussion, so she had an MRI this morning."

A male nurse comes into the room. "Wake up. Wake up, Ms. Walsh," he says.

I tilt my head. Those words. My breath quickens. Being back in the hospital is probably triggering me. I've got to stay calm. It's not about me—it's about Bri. I need to be strong.

"I need to check how you're doing, Brianna," the nurse says.

I move to her bed and touch her arm lightly. "Wake up, babe."

"Ren?" Bri says, her voice dry.

"Bri, I'm here." I move a strand of hair off her forehead.

She opens her eyes and blinks. "Ren? Is that you?"

"Yes." I rub her cheek. "I'm here."

"I wanted to call you, but the nurse couldn't find my phone." She points to the male nurse standing next to the bed.

The nurse explains, "I told her to rest and I would go to the ER and ask if they found a phone."

"He brought it back about half an hour ago and gave it to me, since Bri wasn't here," Sarah says, "and I called you."

"Thank you. I'm so glad you did. I was worried."

The nurse says, "Here, can you please take your pain medication?" He drops the pills in Bri's hand and moves the small cup of water toward her mouth.

His voice...I've heard it before. But where? I take the cup and read his hospital ID badge, *B. Collins*. I sense the nurse staring at me.

"I'll do it. Thanks. Come on, Bri, take your meds."

She puts the pills in her mouth as I raise the cup to Bri's lips. She takes a sip of the water and swallows.

"What is the medication?" Sarah asks.

"Toradol. It's an anti-inflammatory to treat pain," the nurse says.

"When can I go home?" Bri asks hoarsely.

"You need to talk to the doctor. She should be stopping by soon with results of your CT scan on your knee," Nurse Collins says.

"What about the MRI?" Sarah asks.

Nurse Collins turns toward the computer. "According to your chart, the MRI showed no concussion."

"Whiplash?" Bri asks. "My neck is stiff and tender."

"A grade one, which is exactly what you just described. But you do have some nasty abrasions, contusions, and lacerations from the airbag and seat belt."

"Yeah. I have a colorful seat belt strap mark across my body and waist. Want to see it?" Bri asks me with a broad smile, starting to lift her covers.

I laugh as the nurse leaves. "Not now. Maybe later."

"Bri, what happened?" Sarah asks.

"I remember stopping at the red light, and out of nowhere, my car lurched forward. Next thing I know, I'm waking up with my head in the airbag."

"Oh, Bri." I kiss her forehead.

There is a knock, and a woman in a white coat over blue scrubs walks in. "Good afternoon, Brianna."

"Hi, Doctor. This is Sarah, my very good friend and business partner. And Renata, my...my—"

"I'm her girlfriend," I quickly respond. I look to Bri. A wide grin appears from ear to ear.

The doctor looks back at Bri. "Well, I'm glad you're both here. You don't have any internal injuries, fractures, or concussion. You do have slight whiplash, but nothing that two days of alternating heat and ice on your neck for fifteen minutes every three hours can't take away. You can use a bag of frozen peas for ice and a heating pad for heat.

"You and the other driver were lucky. He was going too fast for the road conditions and was on his phone. He braked a bit too late."

"When can I go home?"

"Tomorrow, late morning. You'll need someone to stay with you for a few days."

"No need to worry about that. I'll be with her," I say, grabbing her hand.

"Wonderful. I'll be by tomorrow to sign you out. Nice meeting everyone."

Bri tries to sit up and says, "Oh, that hurts."

I go over and put my hand on her back and move her pillow behind her.

"Thank you. How did you find me?"

Sarah looks at me sympathetically. "I'm sorry I didn't call sooner. My phone ran out of juice. I gave it to the kids last night to play a game. This morning I answered the call from the hospital and didn't realize the charge was low so when I arrived at the hospital, the battery was dead. I called you as soon as the nurse brought back Bri's phone."

"It's okay. We're here, and you"—I point to Bri—"are going home tomorrow." I hug her.

"Ouch."

"Sorry." I gently rest my head on her shoulder. "I was so worried."

"I'm going to be fine. Probably later than sooner," Bri chuckles.

Sarah and I stay for another hour until we notice Bri's eyes start to close. Nurse Collins comes back in to check on her.

"Bri, honey, Sarah and I are going to leave." I take her hand and kiss her forehead.

"Ren."

"Yes?"

She reaches her hand to my face and caresses my cheek. She can hardly keep her eyes open. I hold her hand to my face.

"I love you," she says.

My breath catches. I lean and whisper in her ear, "I love you too."

CHAPTER SIXTY

As I pack to stay at Bri's on Sunday morning, the voices from last night's dream keep popping into my head. I have the nagging sensation that someone is tapping my head, trying to get me to remember something, and it won't stop.

I survey the top of my bed to make sure I have everything. I spot my phone charger and throw it in between my blue jeans and fleece jacket. I drag my suitcase to the living room, where I gather my Christmas break catch-up folders from the breakfast table and stash them in my briefcase.

My phone rings. I hope Bri is calling to tell me to pick her up early. "Bri?"

"No. Me," the stalker's voice says.

"Stop calling me."

"Your girlfriend will not be waking up this morning. Now we can be together."

I recognize that voice. That one telling me to wake up in my dream.

"Oh, God, Bri." My briefcase falls out of my other hand, and folders spill out onto the floor. I speed-dial the police.

"Sergeant Jackson."

"Officer, this is Renata Santos. Bri is—he's going to hurt Bri. The same voice. My dream. The voice on my phone. The nurse's voice—"

"Renata, slow down."

"I—you have to get to the hospital!"

"Why?"

I run into my garage, jump in my car and start the engine. "My dreams—the voice is the same voice of Bri's nurse, Brent Collins, at Miami Valley Hospital. He just called and said, 'Your girlfriend will not be waking up this morning. Now we can be together.'"

"Brent Collins. Renata—that's the name of the man identified by the candy store." I hear Sergeant Jackson yell, "Possible suspect, Brent Collins, nurse at Miami Valley Hospital. Go. Go." Then she says to me, "We have officers on their way, and my partner is calling hospital security now."

I'm breathless. "How did you get his name?"

"The person at the candy store remembered a man who got agitated and rude when he needed to use his credit card. And he is on their CCTV—we traced the card to Brent Collins. You said he threatened your girlfriend? I gotta go."

I put my car in reverse, I gaze into my rearview mirror and realize my garage door is still down. I hit my steering wheel with both hands and tell myself to calm down. Deep breath. The police are heading to the hospital, and security has been notified.

CHAPTER SIXTY-ONE

I race through the hospital entrance and hit the elevator button multiple times. As I stand and wait impatiently, I press the button three more times.

An older lady next to me I didn't even notice says, "No use pushing that button. It'll get here in its sweet old time."

My heart is racing. I can't lose Bri. I shift my weight back and forth. As I contemplate taking the stairs, the bell rings and the elevator door opens.

The woman and I jump in. *God, hurry*, I say to myself as I hold the door from closing on her as another person quickly jumps in behind her and says, "Thanks. Fourth floor, please."

"Me too," the woman says.

I sigh, relieved we're not stopping before we get to the third floor. I lower my head into my hands. Please, Bri, be all right.

The door closes, and the elevator doesn't move. I hit the button again and say out loud, "Come on!" Sweat is running down my back.

The woman reaches out and touches my arm. "Honey, you looked stressed. Whatever is going on, you got to believe everything is going to be all right."

Finally, the elevator moves. I whisper, "I pray you're right."

The elevator finally opens on the third floor, and I sprint down the hall to Bri's room, dodging nurses, trolleys, and service carts. When I turn the corner, Sergeant Jackson and two officers escort a handcuffed Nurse Collins from Bri's room.

I stop inches from him, my body shaking. "Why?" I whisper.

His face twists. "You don't remember."

My hands form fists. "No. I don't."

"Renata," Sergeant Jackson says as she steps between us and gently nudges me back two steps.

"I was your nurse when you were in the hospital."

No. *No.* "I had a lot of nurses."

"But I'm the one who comforted you through your painful surgeries. I'm the one who held your hand and told you everything was going to be okay."

My face grows hot with anger, and my fingernails burrow into my palms. "I don't remember."

His eyes become hopeful. "You thanked me for being by your side and said we would be together forever."

"What are you talking about?" I hiss. "I was so out of it with pain medication. I didn't recognize who I was talking to or what I was saying."

"That's why I sent you the flowers and candy. You told me you liked flowers and candy."

"I don't remember saying that, but I do remember your voice telling me to wake up. In my dream."

He takes a step toward me, and the officers pull him back as he says, "Well, I remember what you said to me. And when I saw you with...her"—he turns his head toward Bri's room—"and you told her you loved her. I couldn't let her *have* you." His voice is tight and enraged.

I stare at him.

Sergeant Jackson touches my shoulder. "Get him out of here," she instructs the officers. "Relax, Ms. Santos. It's over."

I unclench my fist and relax my arms. "I need to see Bri."

I rush into the room. Bri sits in her bed, her head resting on the pillow. Bri opens her arms, and I fall into them.

We cry softly together, a cry of relief.

CHAPTER SIXTY-TWO

We walk through Bri's front door on Monday morning, Bri using a cane to support her bruised knee. I guide her into the living room and say, "Come on. Let's get you on the couch."

"I'm so glad to be home."

I hold her arm as she settles in with a groan. I grab both her legs and place them lengthwise on the couch. She puts her cane on the floor next to the sofa.

Leaning on the arm of the couch, she says, "I could have been home yesterday if not for all the drama with Mr. Collins."

"You call him threatening you *drama*? Bri, when I got that call from him, his message was clear—he did not want you around." I cringe.

Bri reaches for my hand. "Ren—"

"No," I say, tears filling my eyes. "It sounded like he wanted to kill you, Bri."

"Right, but security got to him first."

Bri closes her eyes and runs her hands through her hair, then looks up at me with matching tears in her eyes and says, "I was scared, too, when I woke up to him saying, 'She will be mine now.' Then security rushed in and grabbed him from behind."

I kneel to the side, resting a hand on her thigh and shoulder. "I was so afraid I was going to lose you."

She reaches for my hand on her thigh and brushes my tears away with the other. "I'm here with you. We're together."

"Yes, together," I repeat, wrapping my arms around her neck and kissing her cheek.

She grabs my hand and brings it to her lips, pressing a soft kiss to my knuckles, and says with a twinkle in her eye, "Together, my girlfriend and me."

I smile. "I like the sound of that." I grab a pillow and place it under her knee. "I'll get the ice."

"Ren." I stop and turn to her. "Ah...thanks for being here with me."

"I wouldn't want to be anywhere else." I smile and head to the freezer. "Here, fifteen minutes."

"That's cold!" Bri takes off the ice pack. "Fifteen minutes? Really?"

"Yes, fifteen minutes. Now suck it up." I move her hand and put the ice pack back on her knee. "Sergeant Jackson will be by this afternoon to review our statements from yesterday."

"And give us an update on the nurse and why he sent you the gifts and why he"—Bri swallows hard—"why he wanted you to himself?"

I squat beside her and squeeze her shoulders. "I don't have an answer. All I know is that you are safe, and we are together."

"Ow, not so tight."

I release my embrace. "Sorry."

"Let me move this way a little so it doesn't hurt so much. This seat belt bruise is impeding our cuddling."

"Do you think you need to call your brother and tell him you're home? They could come to visit later this week," I say, putting a pillow behind Bri's back.

"Okay, I'll call him now. Where's my phone?"

"Ah...I believe it's in your back pocket."

She lifts and touches her ass cheek, smiles, and says, "Yeah. Got it," then dials the number. "Hello, David? Yes, I'm okay. Well, as okay as one can be after being rear-ended."

Laughter echoes from the phone.

"No, Renata is here with me. Yeah, sounds great. I'll see you and Liz Thursday. Bye, David."

"It will be good to see them again."

"Yes, it will." Bri touches my hand and squeezes it.

I sit at the other end of the couch, take off Bri's shoes and socks, and rub her feet.

"Oh, that feels *so* good."

"Can I ask you something?"

"Sure."

"The other day, when I was leaving your room, do you remember what you said to me?"

"You mean when you bent over to say goodbye?"

I blush. "Yeah."

She smiles. "Ah…yes. I do."

"Did you mean what you said"—I lock onto her blue eyes—"or was it the medication?"

"You mean, did I mean it when I said I love you?"

I stop rubbing her feet. "Yeah."

Bri wiggles her finger to come to her. With a groan, she swings her feet onto the floor. She taps her hand on the couch for me to sit next to her.

Then she turns to face me and touches my cheek with her open hand. "Yes. Absolutely. Renata Santos, I am in love with you." She reaches to wrap her arms around my shoulder but winces. "Ouch. I can't reach around you. It hurts."

I grab both of her hands and place them in my lap. "Did you hear what I said back?"

"Yes, right before I fell asleep. You told me you loved me."

"I did. And yes, I love you, Bri."

"And I love you, Renata," she says, "and I want to show you how much. But I can't move my arms without it hurting."

"I can wait." I smile and kiss Bri on her cheek.

CHAPTER SIXTY-THREE

We sit on the living room couch, Sergeant Jackson on an adjacent chair.

"What can you tell us about Mr. Collin's motivation?" I ask.

"Well, six months ago, his girlfriend died of horrific burn injuries from a car accident. Remember that pileup on the interstate that involved fifteen cars and five tractor trailers. She was in the car that caught fire. Naturally, he was devastated, and took a lengthy leave of absence. When he finally returned to work, he asked to be reassigned out of the burn unit because, not surprisingly, he found it too distressing. But it appears he became fixated on burn patients who were previously under his care. And the director of nursing told me he wasn't even supposed to be on duty the day we arrested him."

I think hard. "I don't remember him. But for some reason, I remembered his voice." I grab Bri's hand. "It was the voice in my dreams."

"After your second report, we started receiving complaints from other burn survivors like you—getting creepy calls, receiving flowers and gifts from an unknown admirer. We finally followed up on your candy and confirmed his identity on the CCTV footage."

"He sent flowers and candy to his girlfriend during their courtship, and I guess he was reliving those days."

"It sounds like he is still dealing with her death," Bri muses.

I think back to my recovery journey and moving from burn victim to survivor. I had Clare, Izzy, Ryan, Darlene, and the Phoenix group. And more recently, Bri. They all gave me the courage to believe in myself again—to believe that I am worthy of love, no matter how my body looks.

"I agree," Sergeant Jackson says.

"Will he receive mental health treatment?" Bri asks.

"I hope so." I look to Bri and then to Sergeant Jackson. "I mean, it doesn't excuse what he's done, but hopefully with some proper help, he can start to heal."

"He will be receiving psychiatric treatment. He's been taken into care, so it finishes here," Sergeant Jackson says, standing. "I have your statements. And along with all your reports, voice messages, that's all the information we need for now. If we need anything else, I'll contact you."

"Thank you," I say.

"Anything else before I leave?"

Bri clears her throat. "Yes. Please thank the security guard for me."

"We are lucky, the security guard got to him as soon as he walked into your room."

I wrap my arm around Bri's shoulder as she releases her breath. "Yes, thank you, security guard."

I lean my head on her shoulder and say, "I second that."

"Thanks, Sergeant," Bri says.

"I'll let myself out."

When the door closes, I turn to Bri, who's staring into space, her eyes unfocused.

I touch her arm. "Are you okay?"

She shakes her head and looks at me. "I could have died *twice*. First in the car accident and again at the hands of the maniac nurse."

"But you didn't die. You survived, like me." I enclose her face with my hands.

Bri covers my hands with hers.

CHAPTER SIXTY-FOUR

Thursday afternoon, I'm in the kitchen making a chocolate cake while Bri sits on the couch. She drops the iPad on her lap and says, "I'm anxious about seeing David and Liz today."

I stop mixing. "Why?"

"I guess it's not about seeing them. I'm concerned about David and his state of mind. When there is stress or anxiety or pressure, it's one of his triggers."

"But, honey, the last time you talked with him about visiting, he was doing well, right?"

"Yeah. His voice sounded fine, but this situation with me, the car accident, the nurse...I'm not sure how he's going to handle it, emotionally speaking."

I draw her into a side hug and kiss her temple. "Have faith in him and Liz. The last time I saw you all together when I intruded"—I give her a half-grin—"he seemed to be headed in the right direction."

Bri leans her head on my shoulder. "I know. I hope he's still following through with his commitment."

"I hope so too." I kiss her head and return to the kitchen to put the cake in the oven.

There's a knock at the door. "That's probably David and Liz," she shouts from the couch.

"I'll get it," I say, turning in time to see her stumble from the couch and start walking toward the door. "Bri! Stop."

"Renata," she says, "my knee is bruised, not broken. I can do it." She hobbles toward the door.

"Where's your cane?"

"On the floor by the couch."

"So why aren't you using it?"

She turns to me and says softly, "I don't need a cane."

I stand with my hands on my hips. "Bri—"

"Renata, it's only a few steps."

I smile. I see myself in Bri, thinking that being injured and needing help is weak. But my journey has taught me that it takes strength and support from others to complete the process. "You're not a very good patient," I say as Bri turns and continues to the door.

I hear her say, "Come on in."

I watch as she hobbles back into the living room, David and Liz following. David asks, "Aren't you supposed to be using a cane?"

"I don't need it."

David reaches out to put his arm around her waist. "Sure looks like it, Hopalong Cassidy."

She pushes his arm away. "David, I don't need your help."

He steps in front of Bri, who stops and glares at him. "I know you're my big sister, but what happened with the nurse…"

Bri straightens and stares at him. "David, I'm fine."

Liz steps around them and joins me in the living room. Shoulder to shoulder, we look at each other and smile, turning back to observe the sibling battle.

David takes a deep breath. "You have always been there for me over the years. Let me help you for once, damn it."

Bri raises her hands in surrender. "Okay. Okay." She turns to me with a smile, and I squeeze Liz's shoulder as David puts his arm around Bri's waist and helps her to the couch.

"What else do you need?" he asks.

"She needs to ice her knee and neck. The peas are in the freezer."

David says, "I'm on it."

CHAPTER SIXTY-FIVE

A week later, we arrive at Clare's to celebrate Christmas. I open the passenger door for Bri. Unfortunately, two inches of snow are still on the ground.

"Thanks, Ren."

I kiss her. "No problem. Tricky walking with your cane."

"I don't need it, you know."

"Yeah, yeah. Just use it for me?"

"Okay, sweetheart."

She eases her way out of the car, and as she walks toward the front door, I ask, "Are you ready to celebrate Christmas with my family?"

"Yes! I've been looking forward to it all week."

"I'll bring in the gifts," I say, motioning for her to continue. My heart aches with happiness I never thought I would experience again, but it also scares me. I struggle with not falling back into victim mode but having Bri by my side makes the journey less frightening.

I carry the bags of presents to the door as Izzy comes flying out, armed with a huge grin. "Merry Christmas!"

She skids to a stop in front of Bri.

"Merry Christmas, Izzy!"

"Can I give you a hug?"

Bri opens her arms. "Sure."

Izzy wraps her arms around her stomach without squeezing. Bri turns to me with a look of puzzlement. "That's the best you can do?"

Izzy gazes up at her in consternation. "I don't want to hurt you."

"You won't. Now, give me your strong Izzy hug."

Izzy smiles and squeezes her.

Bri glances at me, wincing, and mouths, *Ouch*. I smile.

"That's the Izzy hug I need."

Finally, Izzy releases her and grabs her hand. "Let me help you!" She guides Bri into the house as I hold the door. As she crosses the threshold, she says, "Watch your step," and grabs Bri's hip to balance her.

"Thank you, Izzy."

We take a few more steps, and then Izzy stops and puts her hands on her hips. "Hey, shouldn't you be using your cane?"

I throw my hands in the air. "Thank you, Izzy!"

Bri looks back and forth between us. "You Santos women are all the same—bossy." She takes a step with the cane, and asks, "Satisfied?"

"Good," Izzy says firmly, grabbing her other hand. "Okay. Come on. I got ya."

"Merry Christmas, everyone," Bri says as we walk into the family room. Christmas music plays in the background, and the tree lights glow in front of the lanai doors, gifts scattered under the tree.

A teary Clare comes up to us.

"Sis, you, okay?" I ask.

"Yes. I'm just so happy to see both of you." She hugs me and then Bri, holding her a bit longer. "I'm glad you are safe," she tells her, and then tells me, "I'm glad your secret admirer is behind bars, or at least out of harm's way."

Ryan comes to us, and we all hug, to which Bri says with a laugh, "Okay, okay. Still a little sore."

"Oh, sorry!" Clare says. We all disengage from the hug.

"Oh, don't be. The pain reminds me I'm alive," Bri says, kissing my cheek.

"Hey, can we open the gifts now?" Izzy asks.

"We talked about this. We're going to eat first, then gifts," Ryan says.

Down the middle of the table is a macrame table runner decorated with fir garlands and a string of lights, surrounded by simple white plates. "Clare, the table is beautiful."

"Thanks, sis." To Bri, Clare explains, "We're having a traditional Portuguese dish called bacalhau com todos. Our grandmother would make it for us at Christmas, so I thought I would try this year."

"It smells delicious. What's in it?" Bri asks.

"It's a simple dish of boiled potatoes, cabbage, eggs, and codfish fillet. You drizzle olive oil on it and add chopped garlic."

"It smells just like Grandma's."

"We're doing buffet style, so grab your plate and fill 'er up."

When Bri grabs her plate and walks with a slight limp and no cane to the counter, I look to Izzy, and we both shake our heads.

We fill our plates, return to the table, and all catch up on our last few days.

"Ren, have you heard about your grant application for the VR project?" Ryan asks after taking his last forkful of bacalhau com todos.

"As a matter of fact, yes. The school got an early Christmas present—our grant application was approved."

"Congrats! That's wonderful," Clare says.

"But then you do have an inside track with the approval process." Ryan smirks and punches Bri on the arm.

"Oh, no, I did not," I say with a laugh. "Bri removed herself from the grant review team. Darlene and I did it on our own merits."

"I wouldn't expect anything else," he says. "Congratulations, Ren. I had no doubt."

Izzy bounces in her chair. "Can we open presents now?"

Clare looks at Ryan, and they both say, "Sure."

We move back to the family room, Bri and I on the couch, Clare and Ryan on chairs to the side of the sofa, and Izzy on her knees on the floor in front of the tree. Her eyes are wide with anticipation.

Clare asks Izzy, "You want to be Santa Claus?"

"Sure." Izzy crawls around the tree and finds a gift. "This one is for you, Bri, from Aunt Ren." She hands it to Bri, who smiles at me and thanks me.

When Bri rips off the wrapping paper, her eyes widen. "Thank you! I've been wanting to read this book."

"What is it?" Izzy asks.

"*My Own Words* about Ruth Bader Ginsburg."

"She was the Supreme Court justice, right?" Izzy asks.

"Right," we all answer in unison.

"I believe there's another gift for Bri," I tell Izzy.

Izzy returns to the tree, pulls out another bag, and reads, "To Bri, from Renata," before handing it to Bri. Bri inspects the bag and pulls out the multicolored tissue paper, sticking her head as close to the top of the bag as she can.

When she raises her head, a huge smile has appeared on her face. She takes out three pairs of socks: one has a donkey on them and says *Smartass*, another has a picture of Ruth Bader Ginsburg, and the last pair say, *I'm a girl. What's your superpower?*

"Thank you. You know the way to my heart." She kisses me. "Izzy, can you bring my bag to me, please? Okay. Let's see." Bri brings out a small rectangular box wrapped in Cleveland Browns wrapping paper and hands it to Izzy, who rips off the wrapping paper and tears open the box.

"Crazy socks!" Izzy yells, holding them up. "I love them! Look—this pair has dolphins, this one has pizzas on it, and the last one has *I heart you* on it." She stands and hugs Bri. "We can be twins. Thank you."

"You're welcome. Okay, who's next?" Bri searches the bag again. "Ryan!" She hands him an envelope.

"You didn't have to…Wow. A two-year subscription to the NFL RedZone and NFL Network. Thanks, Bri."

Back in the bag again, Bri retrieves another envelope, hands it to Clare, and says, "For you."

"A certificate for a spa day!"

"Yeah, it includes a massage, pedicure, manicure, and lots more. You deserve a day just for you."

"That is so thoughtful. Thank you."

"And last but not least"—Bri reaches back into the bag—"this is for you." She hands me what looks like a small container wrapped in Santa Claus wrapping paper.

"Just what I needed!" I hold up the container. "A five-pound jar of peanut M&M's."

Izzy asks, "Will you share?"

"You bet I will."

Bri reaches back into the bag and hands me an envelope.

"Come on, Aunt Ren," Izzy urges, "open it."

I do so, and my jaw drops. "Bri, these are plane tickets to New York! And Broadway play tickets to *Wicked*!"

"You said you'd never been, and we talked about going to New York."

"Bri. I'm speechless." I embrace her and whisper in her ear, "I love you."

"I love *you*. I think there's another envelope in the bag." She hands the bag to Izzy and asks, "Can you look for me?"

Izzy takes the bag and sticks her hand inside. "It says Izzy, from Bri." She looks puzzled. "But you already gave me the socks."

"Yeah, but you're the best receiver on our team, so you deserve more than one gift."

Izzy looks to her father, her eyes filled with anticipation. Ryan says, "Open it."

Her eyes are the size of quarters when she turns to Clare and Ryan. "Mom! Dad! I think—I think—a plane ticket, and this says *Wicked*!"

I turn to Bri with a huge smile.

"Yeah. The three of us are going to New York in June after you're both out of school."

I turn to Ryan and Clare. "You knew about this trip?"

"Sure. Bri asked us, and we said fine."

Izzy crashes into Bri, throwing her arms around her neck. "Thank you. I've never been on a plane."

"Izzy, be careful," Clare says.

Bri puts up her hand and shakes her head, signaling she's okay. "I thought it would be fun for you, Aunt Ren, and me to go together."

"Thank you, thank you! Wait till I tell Ashley!"

I hug Bri. She is so thoughtful and kind. How did I get so lucky?

"Um...is there one more? One for Bri?" Clare asks Izzy.

Izzy jumps off Bri and crawls under the tree, her legs sticking out comically. "It's here somewhere. Wait, I think I see it—yep, got it." Izzy hands Bri the envelope. "Here, this is for you from the Randolph family. That's us—Mom, Dad, Aunt Ren, and me."

"Go ahead. Open it," Clare says.

Smiling, Bri opens it and pulls out a single sheet of paper. Her eyes move over the paper.

Izzy jumps up and down. "Read what it says!"

I am nervous. I hope I haven't gone overboard. After all, we all discussed the gift as a family and agreed.

Bri clears her throat. "This is a lifetime invitation, signed by all of you"—she makes eye contact with each of us—"to your Sunday dinners."

"You brought back the sparkle in my sister's eyes," Clare says.

"We want you to be part of our family," Ryan adds.

Bri looks at me, eyes filled with tears. "Now *I'm* speechless."

I hold her face in my hands. "Bri, I want you in my life for a lifetime."

"I want *you* in my life," she says, placing a gentle kiss on my lips.

Someone taps our shoulders. "Okay, okay." Izzy stands in front of us. "Stop kissing because there is one stipulation. I just learned that word."

Bri clears her throat. "What's the stipulation?"

"You must be on my team when we play football because you pass better than Dad."

"Deal." Bri gives Izzy a high five.

CHAPTER SIXTY-SIX

I pack my bags the following morning as Bri leans on the bedroom doorjamb.

"I know you have to go and prepare for the next semester, but—"

I fold a pair of jeans and gently arrange them in my suitcase, wondering what Bri will say next. I have no idea what she's thinking. I turn as she steps through the threshold. Her pink, red, and purple bruises from the airbag and seat belt are fading.

"But?" I ask.

She reaches me and grabs my hands. "But—uh—thanks for taking care of me." She smirks. "I could get used to you hanging around here more."

"Oh, you could?" I wrap my arms around her neck.

She lowers her head and rocks from side to side.

"Bri? What is it?"

She lifts her head, tears in her eyes.

My hands move to her face. "What is it?"

"I'm scared I'm not going to see you again." She places one hand over mine. "I think back to the nutjob nurse standing over me. I think I'm having a delayed reaction." She breaks away from our embrace and walks toward the window, her back to me.

I race to her and surround her in my arms. Her body is tense, her breathing shallow and rapid. "But he didn't. We're together." I kiss her neck. "And he is not going to hurt anyone again."

I've never seen Bri so vulnerable and anxious. She's always been the strong one. Now it's my turn to hold her and be strong for her.

I squeeze her tightly. "Sergeant Jackson told us he's being transferred to a psychiatric hospital." I kiss her neck again. "If you like, I'll call her tomorrow."

Her shoulders relax, and her breathing slowly returns to normal. "No. I'll be fine."

I turn Bri around in my arms and touch my forehead to hers. "And you will see me again. We have a date for New Year's Eve with your partners at Rays Restaurant, remember? And afterward"—I wiggle my eyebrows—"we'll make up for lost time."

"Yeah." She smiles. "I only hope I can stay awake till midnight."

"You and me both." We laugh, and I go back and close my suitcase.

As Bri walks me out, she wraps her arm around my waist. I've felt safe in her arms since the first time we slept together, the night I had my nightmare and she held me. I don't want to lose this feeling.

I drop my suitcase and hug her with all my might. "I love you, Brianna Walsh. I guess the one good thing that came out of this whole thing is that I finally told you I love you."

She squeezes me, her hands rubbing my back. "I miss your touch."

"Well, it hasn't been easy lying next to you and not jumping your bones."

She laughs. "Tell me about it. The other night when I made an attempt, my ribs wouldn't allow me to finish."

"It was a good attempt. Your kiss on my neck and moving down my collarbone…"

"And then when I moved to top you, ouch—and then I collapsed on my back."

We stare into each other's eyes. And then our lips are crashing into each other, sending electricity down to my toes. Her hands roaming down my back, Bri moans in my ear, "To hell with my injuries." My breath catches as her hands squeeze my ass.

"I can't wait until New Year's Eve," I say between our mutual moaning, and then I think better of waiting. I grab her hand and lead her back to the bedroom. "To hell with preparing. It can wait."

CHAPTER SIXTY-SEVEN

As we walk into my house after celebrating New Year's Eve, Bri flops onto the couch. "We made it."

I collapse beside her. "Yes, we did. And your kiss at midnight, well…" I lean over her and kiss her, nipping her lower lip before breaking our kiss to leave a trail of kisses across her jaw. Slowly, I lick her ear. "I have a surprise for you."

Through ragged breaths, Bri gasps, "You do?"

I stand, grab her hands, and pull her up so our bodies crash together and I kiss her parted lips, my tongue rocketing into her mouth.

Bri moans, and my heart pounds as I run my hand over her breast and down her stomach. My hand continues to the apex of her thighs.

She rocks her hips into my hand. "Jesus, Renata."

"Yes?" I add pressure to my stroke.

"Um—what's the surprise?"

I remove my hand and look directly into her eyes. "Go to the bedroom, turn on the lamp by the bed, undress, lie under the covers and wait for me."

Bri's eyes widen. "You turn me on so much when you take charge and tell me what to do, you know that?"

I grin. "I know." I point toward the bedroom. "Now go!"

Bri begins with a sprint but after three strides, grabs her knee and slows down on her way to the bedroom as I follow her, but I turn left at the guest bedroom.

I smile as I undress, admiring myself in the full-length mirror. I run my hands down my body and swivel from side to side, my eyes taking in all of me—the whole picture, including my scars. I never imagined I'd feel confident enough in my body to wear seductive lingerie.

The red lace bra set includes underwire peek-a-boo cups and eyelash trim, a garter belt with straps holding up thigh-high lace stockings, and a matching thong. Now all I have to do is slide my feet into three-inch red stilettos and hope I don't fall when I make my entrance.

I take one last look. I want Bri to know she is loved and how much I cherish her. After tonight, I hope she knows she's the one I want to be with for a lifetime.

I take a deep breath and walk to the master bedroom. When I swing open the door, Bri is leaning against the headboard, the sheet tucked under her armpits, covering her chest.

I lean against the doorway, hand on the doorframe.

Bri's mouth falls open, her eyes wide. Her mouth moves, but nothing comes out. The covers fall, revealing breasts waiting to be devoured.

I take two careful steps forward as Bri's mouth opens and closes silently. I reach the foot of the bed and turn slowly, my back toward her, ass cheeks in full view. I glance over my shoulder as Bri finally says, "Oh my." She licks her lips. "Oh my."

I face her. The soft lamplight from the lamp illuminates her glorious breasts.

"Renata...I...you are...wow. You are sexy as hell."

I strut to the side of the bed, and Bri reaches for me. I hold up my hands. "No. Tonight is all about you, my love."

I throw the covers off, her naked body sending warmth from my chest to my toes. I return to the foot of the bed and pull her by ankles till her head is on the pillow.

"Renata, please, my temperature is about to reach its boiling point." She leans up on her elbows. "Your outfit—it's driving me crazy."

I spread her legs. "That's the idea." I crawl between her legs and work my way up her body, occasionally kissing her thighs, stomach, and breasts, making sure the lace grazes her hot skin until I'm only inches away from her lips. "Tonight, you"—I run my tongue over her lower lip—"are all mine."

Our lips crash together with a passion I never thought possible. Bri's hands roam uncontrollably over my body, oblivious to my scars. God, I love her.

I break our kiss and take a breath. "Remember"—I kiss her neck—"you"—I kiss her breast—"are"—I slide down and run my tongue over her pubic hairline—"mine."

As I dive into the abyss of her beauty, Bri moans, "I'm yours."

EPILOGUE

I stand in front of our full-length mirror, scars exposed, and think back over the past year.

Bri's business grew, which required her to be gone for weeks at a time. Those days of waiting were filled with my anticipation of being with her, whether sitting on the couch cuddling, hiking, reading, biking on the bike path, cluttering the kitchen, or gazing at the full moon.

No matter how long she was gone, the lovemaking upon her return—the passion, the intensity—reinforced our love for one another.

We had dinner with David and Liz at least once a month, and they joined us at Clare and Ryan's for Sunday dinner every now and then. David continued attending his AA meetings and received rave reviews at his job. His life was firmly on track.

Our trip to New York City was fabulous. Izzy was overwhelmed by the lights and billboards on Times Square, and she was so entranced with *Wicked* that we had to listen to the soundtrack whenever we were in the car with her.

The new school year brought VR into the classroom, and to my delight, both teachers and students reported renewed interest and improved grades in the science department. Our STEM scores skyrocketed. As a result, we will expand VR into the history department next year.

Darlene got the vice principal position at Valley View. Shelly moved up to Ohio to be with her, and they will be moving into their new home in January. And we double-date as often as we can.

I had two more laser surgeries, one on my arm and one on my hip. Bri was right there by my side and never once turned away from me or my scars. I continue to attend my support group, and we also attend a quarterly online group for couples.

When I stare at my reflection, I see me, my scars, and my heart. I place my open hand over it and say, "I see you. I see all of you."

I finish dressing, meet Bri in the dining room, and help her set the table. Around two, the front door opens, and Izzy bursts into Bri's house—now our house, as I moved in with her upon returning from our New York City adventure.

"Merry Christmas, Aunt Ren and Aunt Bri," Izzy says, skidding to a stop in the foyer while Ryan holds the door for Clare. There is a honk as David and Liz pull into the driveway.

Ryan waves from the porch.

"Merry Christmas, Izzy," Bri responds, embracing her.

Izzy pulls on her arm so she'll bend down, then she whispers something into her ear.

Clare sees her daughter and says, "Izzy got up this morning at dawn, dressed and ready to come here. In the car, she told Ryan to drive faster—and now this."

Bri holds Izzy's hand and leads her into the hallway by the bedrooms.

"Where are you two going?" Clare yells. "David and Liz are here."

"I want to show something to Izzy," Bri calls. "I'll be right back."

"Here, give me your coats," I say. "Everyone, please come in and make yourselves at home."

As they all walk in, I overhear Ryan say to David, "You know, the past two weeks, those two have been acting strange."

"They must know something we don't," David replies.

I return from hanging up the coats and hug David and Liz. "Even in New York, they acted like they were keeping a secret from me. They even went shopping one afternoon without me."

"Really?" Clare asks.

"Yeah. Anyway." I shake my head. "I'm sure Bri is showing Izzy the new socks she got for Christmas from her partners."

"Bri and her socks. Now Izzy won't wear anything but flashy socks," Clare laughs, then her look softens. "Ren, you look happy."

I gaze around the room, surrounded by people who care about me and whom I get to call family. "I am happy." The timer sounds, so I go to check the turkey. I don't even flinch at the oven's heat. "Thirty minutes until we eat," I announce, "and now I can use some help to heat up all the side dishes."

"The turkey smells wonderful," Liz says.

Bri and Izzy return, all smiles and giggles.

I give Bri a puzzled face, to which she says, "Never mind," and winks at me. As she passes me in the kitchen, she kisses my cheek and asks, "Anything I can do?"

"Yes, kiss me again."

As she does, Liz slaps my shoulder and jokes, "Okay, you two. Enough. Some of us are hungry!"

After we've eaten and the dishes are in the dishwasher, we gather around the brightly lit tree to exchange gifts.

Izzy sits on her knees and asks, "Can I be Santa Claus again?"

"Of course, sweetie," Clare says.

Izzy picks up a gift and reads the tag, "To David, from Bri." David starts to unwrap his gift, but before he can finish, Izzy gives a gift to Clare, then hands the next one to Liz before Clare can unwrap hers.

"Whoa, slow down! You're handing out the presents too fast. We don't have time to show everyone what we got before you hand out the next one," Clare says gently.

Izzy rocks from side to side, looking at Bri, who gestures for her to calm down. Clare and I glance at each other.

"What are you two up to?" she asks suspiciously.

Her eyes big and her arms flapping up and down like a giant bird, Izzy asks Bri, "Now?"

I ask, "What's going on?"

Bri gets up and says to Izzy, "Yeah. Now."

Izzy bolts down the bedroom hall and returns with an envelope in one hand, her other hand holding something tucked under her shirt. She hands the envelope to Bri, who passes it to me. "Merry Christmas, Renata."

I pull out a certificate.

I notice Izzy hand something to Bri. Liz gasps.

"Read it," Clare says.

"Yeah, read it," David says.

I unfold the paper, flip it over a few times and say, "It looks like the lifetime certificate we gave Bri last year."

"What does it say?" Liz asks.

I clear my throat and read, "'Renata. You made me believe and trust in love again. You enrich my life with your love and passion.'" I stop and glance up at Bri.

"Go on," Izzy says, waving her hands.

I continue, "'You make every day an adventure.'" Then I read the following sentence to myself and blush. "'You're incredibly sexy.'"

Izzy covers her mouth and laughs.

"'My heart is full of love with you in my life.'"

"Go on. Keep reading," Bri says.

I keep reading. "'I want you in my life for a lifetime.'"

Just then, I look up to see Bri opening a small black ring box. I turn to Clare and Ryan—Clare with tears in her eyes, Ryan with the broadest smile—then David and Liz, who are holding hands. Izzy jumps up and down. "I helped Aunt Bri pick it out in New York!"

Bri reaches for my hand, her intense blue eyes meeting mine. "Renata Santos, the love of my life, will you marry me for a lifetime?" She holds an emerald ring.

I close my eyes to soak up the moment, then stare at the ring and back into Bri's eyes.

"Well, what do you say?" Izzy asks excitedly.

"I say…yes!"

Bri's face lights up like Times Square as she slides the ring on my finger.

We stand, my arms wrapped around her neck. I lean in and whisper again, "Yes." I get the most tender and passionate kiss in return.

"I told Aunt Bri you would say yes," Izzy crows, hugging us both around our waists.

Clare, Ryan, David, and Liz surround us, and I celebrate the best Christmas ever with a family hug.

I whisper into Bri's ear, "For a lifetime."

Bella Books, Inc.
Women. Books. Even Better Together.

P.O. Box 10543
Tallahassee, FL 32302
Phone: (800) 729-4992
www.BellaBooks.com

More Titles from Bella Books

Mabel and Everything After – Hannah Safren
978-1-64247-390-2 | 274 pgs | paperback: $17.95 | eBook: $9.99
A law student and a wannabe brewery owner find that the path to a fairy tale happily-ever-after is often the long and scenic route.

To Be With You – TJ O'Shea
978-1-64247-419-0 | 348 pgs | paperback: $19.95 | eBook: $9.99
Sometimes the choice is between loving safely or loving bravely.

I Dare You to Love Me – Lori G. Matthews
978-1-64247-389-6 | 292 pgs | paperback: $18.95 | eBook: $9.99
An enemy-to-lovers romance about daring to follow your heart, even when it's the hardest thing to do.

The Lady Adventurers Club - Karen Frost
978-1-64247-414-5 | 300 pgs | paperback: $18.95 | eBook: $9.99
Four women. One undiscovered Egyptian tomb. One (maybe) angry Egyptian goddess. What could possibly go wrong?

Golden Hour - Kat Jackson
978-1-64247-397-1 | 250 pgs | paperback: $17.95 | eBook: $9.99
Life would be so much easier if Lina were afraid of something basic—like spiders—instead of something significant. Something like real, true, healthy love.

Schuss – E. J. Noyes
978-1-64247-430-5 | 276 pgs | paperback: $17.95 | eBook: $9.99
They're best friends who both want something more, but what if admitting it ruins the best friendship either of them have had?